CANDY BOMBERS

Candy Bombers
Copyright © 2006 by Robert Elmer

Requests for information should be addressed to:
Zonderkidz, *Grand Rapids, Michigan* 49530

Library of Congress Cataloging-in-Publication Data

Elmer, Robert.
      Candy bombers / Robert Elmer.
          p. cm.–(The wall series ; bk. 1)
          Summary: In 1948 Berlin, Germany, while trying to survive the Russian blockade of the city and also grieving for his father and sister who were killed in the war, thirteen-year-old Erich is befriended by a United States airman.
          ISBN 978-0-310-70943-5
          1. Berlin (Germany)--History—Blockade, 1948-1949—Juvenile fiction. [1. Berlin (Germany)—History—Blockade, 1948-1949--Fiction. 2. Germany—History—1945-1955—Fiction. 3. Survival—Fiction. 4. Grief--Fiction. 5. Christian life—Fiction.] I. Title.
      PZ7.E4794Can 2006
      [Fic]—dc22

                                         2005032137

Published in association with the literary agency of Alive Communications, Inc., 7680 Goddard Street, Suite. 200, Colorado Springs, CO 80920. www.alivecommunications.com

Editor: Kristen Tuinstra
Art direction: Merit Alderink
Cover design: Jay Smith of Juicebox Design
Interior design: Ruth Bandstra
Interior composition: Ruth Bandstra

Printed in the United States of America

08 09 10 11 12 13 14 • 11 10 9 8 7 6 5

THE WALL

CANDY BOMBERS

ROBERT ELMER

ZONDER**kidz**

ZONDERVAN.com/
AUTHORTRACKER
follow your favorite authors

CONTENTS

PROLOGUE

Nick held Trouble's collar and scanned the runway on the other side of the chain-link fence, just to be sure. From here the Bighorn County Airport looked tons bigger than any old Wyoming airstrip. Maybe because it had started out as a military air base in the 1940s before it became a home for smoke-jumping and forest-firefighting planes. It stretched way out past Little Dry Creek, like a big city airport, only Greybull was no big city.

He counted a dozen bright orange planes parked around the oversized hangars. They used those planes during fire season, not April. And not on a Saturday morning, when the mechanics and everybody else were probably sleeping in.

Then he squinted at the five old cargo planes, their aluminum skins glimmering with the first rays of morning sun. The one on the end was the coolest—a mothballed four-engine C-54 Skymaster transport with a silly flying baby painted on its side. The *Berlin Baby*. Funny name for a plane. But all the planes still wore their stars proudly, even though the years of blistering seasons in Wyoming had faded the old girls.

"Come on, Trouble." He crouched as low as he could and sprinted to the shadow of the C-54's wings. He waited for a moment to make sure nobody saw them. Okay. In one smooth move Nick pulled himself up the rope ladder and swung inside the open hatch of the big Skymaster.

Trouble barked as soon as he disappeared, the way she always did. As in, *Don't forget me!*

"Shh!" Nick tried to quiet her down as he added his pack to his book stash. He took in a whiff of air still smelling of clouds with a hint of airplane fuel. Just right. And that was probably the best part about this place: the smells and the wondering and the dreaming. How many times had she been around the world, and how many miles had slipped under her wings? What kinds of cargoes had filled her huge dark insides, now littered with ripped nets, ropes, and lumpy canvas tarps? And who had flown her during the past forty years, before Nick had secretly taken over command?

Next came Trouble; Nick reached down to the clothes-line still knotted to his belt. He had tied the other end around his little mutt's body like a harness, and it was no trouble to hoist his cargo into the plane with him. The dog had done this dozens of times. So once inside, Trouble curled up in her usual spot behind the co-pilot's chair while Nick secured the hatch and settled into the pilot's seat. He imagined that his view of the distant snowcapped Bighorn Mountains to the east might look almost the same if they were airborne. *Let's take it up to thirty-two thousand. Throttle up. Heading oh-eight-niner.* Trouble glanced up and wagged her tail, thunk-thunking the plane's metal skin. At the same time, a much louder thunk nearly lifted Nick out of his seat.

"Hey, you in there!" *Bam-bam-bam.* "Out! Get out!"

The hair on the back of Trouble's neck stiffened, and she tilted her head at the noise. But with Nick's hand on her collar she didn't bark.

"Good girl," he whispered.

"Do you hear me?" came the foghorn voice again. *Bam-bam-bam.* "Get out of there, or I'm gonna call the sheriff and have you arrested for trespassing."

He would too. Nick had heard the stories about the care-taker. So, like a pilot with a pre-flight checklist, Nick ticked off his options:

Option One: Surrender and come out. Pray for mercy. Hmm. Maybe not.

Option Two: Sit right there and say nothing. But the first place the sheriff would look for him was right there. Which left him with—

Option Three: Hide in the cargo hold. *Really* hide.

"Don't make me wait all day, kid. I know you're in one of these planes."

Aha! *One* of these planes? If the old guy wasn't sure which one, Nick knew he still had a chance of not being discovered. So he slipped off his shoes, picked up Trouble, and tiptoed into the shadowy belly of the airplane. The flashlight gave him a wimpy little flicker, but it still had just enough juice to guide him back past the navigator's table to the cargo hold.

But where to hide? He crawled to the line of wooden crew seats, wedged himself below one, covered himself up with a piece of canvas, and waited.

"Come on, kid!" The voice sounded a little softer this time, moving away. Nick lay back in his hiding place with the bottom of a fold-down wooden seat just inches from his face. And he noticed something.

What's that? He pointed the light up to check it out. Somebody had carved a name into the bottom of the seat. Well, that was rude. But kids did that to old school desks all the time.

Was it really a name, though? Maybe, if you could see past the little stain, which looked like old dried blood. First came a capital *E*, then an *R*, except it was squiggly and hard to make out.

Erich something? The rest of the words didn't look English.

What kind of weird graffiti was that for an old Air Force cargo plane?

1

KAPITEL EINS

BERLIN, GERMANY

Erich stopped his carving for a minute, listening to everything going on outside the plane. So far his plan was going *almost* the way he'd hoped.

Step one, sneak onto the American plane that was unloading supplies at Berlin's Tempelhof Airport. That had been no problem with all the confusion of the airlift—with hundreds of planes coming and going all day and night. In fact, the British and the Americans had been flying in for weeks, ever since the Russians had blocked off Berlin, surrounding it so no supplies could come in or go out by land.

Step two, find a stash of food. Maybe some dried fruit or flour. A few potatoes. Whatever. The Americans would never miss it. They weren't doing this because they cared about the people of Berlin, *nein*. No, Erich was sure of it. It was just part of their war, this *cold* war they fought, the English and the Americans and the French, against the Russians.

Step three, slip away without getting captured by the enemy. And if he could pull this off, everyone back in the neighborhood would call him a hero. Erich the Hero. He liked the sound of that. See? The world war might have been over for three years, but thirteen-year-olds could still do risky—and important—things.

But this plane held no food, nothing. So he decided he'd just leave some kind of record behind. Proof that he'd been here, that he'd been brave enough to do what he'd told everyone he would. Maybe his cousin Katarina and the others would never see it, but he would know, and that would be enough. Keeping one eye on the exit, just in case, he crouched low and used the dull point of his penknife to carve a few words into the bottom of the wooden seat.

And no, he didn't feel guilty, or like a vandal, though Katarina would have yelled at him. After all, this airplane belonged to the enemy. Even though the war had ended, the men who flew this plane had rained fire and death on his city.

And on his family.

And on his father.

Yes, Erich Becker was here to try to even the score, any way he could. Even when the knife slipped and jabbed his finger. *Ouch!* Forget the trickle of blood; he continued for a couple more minutes until he had finished. There. He folded up his knife, crawled to the exit door, and looked around. All clear? He slipped out and landed like a cat on the hard-packed airport runway.

Safe for now. Erich adjusted his cap down lower and wished for a few more shadows so he could blend into the German work crews—men who swarmed over each incoming plane to pick it clean of cargo. No one seemed to notice when he hurried along with everyone else. A truck screeched by him, full of men on their way to unload an approaching C-54. Its pilot followed close behind a guide jeep bearing a big FOLLOW ME sign. If nothing else, the Americans knew how to run an airport.

"Let's go, gentlemen!" A man in uniform windmilled his right arm at the approaching truck, pointing to a place on the pavement where he wanted the work crew to wait. Another man wearing dark green coveralls and white gloves stood at attention in front of the plane parade, directing the latest arrival with twirling hand motions. The plane taxied into position, its four propellers spun down, and the side hatch popped open—all at once. Erich tried not to stare at the finely tuned ballet, where each dancer knew just when to jump, and how high.

Instead, he studied the pavement and held on to his hat as a final gust of propeller backwash hit him, hunched his shoulders, and did his best to look ten years older and six inches taller. Only, which plane would have food in it? Which could he try next? Not the one at the end of the lineup, where the crew raced to unload bin after bin of coal. He skirted around that one while still trying to look as if he were going somewhere on purpose. And that might have worked fine, if he hadn't rounded the next plane … and run square into a brown-uniformed soldier.

"Bitte, bitte." Erich choked out an apology as he caught his balance. "Excuse me."

But that wasn't enough for the soldier, who grabbed Erich by the shirtsleeve and waved a friend over to join them.

"Bitte bitte nothing." The soldier scowled and didn't loosen his grip. "You can't be wandering around here. Which crew are you with, anyway?"

Erich tried to back away, couldn't, and decided the safest answer would be rapid-fire German. He was going over to the *flughafen,* headquarters just as ordered, he said. In a terrible hurry. *Schnell!* But the soldier only held up his free hand, motioning for him to stop.

"Whoa, whoa. Around here we speak English, fella. *Verstehen?* Understand?" He looked a little closer, and his eyes widened. "Hey, wait a minute."

This time Erich did everything he could to wiggle away, twist out of the grip. But the more he tried to flee, the tighter the man squeezed his arm.

"Hey, Andy!" That must have been his friend, now trotting over to join them. "Look at this. This ain't no worker. I just caught me a street kid! How do you think he snuck in here?"

Erich knew he was dead. Take him back to the *kirchof,* the graveyard next to the airport, and bury him.

"Beats me," answered Andy, a dark-skinned man wearing dark green coveralls and a baseball cap with the bill turned up in front. "But you better get him out of here before the captain finds out, or we're going to have some explaining to do."

"Yeah." The first man frowned again and began to drag Erich toward the main terminal building. "You speak English, kid?"

Erich wasn't sure he should answer yes. But he couldn't help staring at the dark soldier as he stumbled away from the airplanes. He'd seen black men before a couple of times, mostly Africans, but only from a distance. Never this close up. Erich had to focus his ears to understand what this man was saying. The edges of the words sounded as if they'd been rounded off, and Erich liked the smooth warmth of them.

"What's the matter, kid?" Andy flashed him a smile. "You look like a deer caught in the headlights."

Erich swallowed hard and nodded, not sure how a deer could find itself in such a place, or he in this one.

"Out this way." The first guy pointed at a gate in the fence where trucks and jeeps came and went past one of the airport's main terminal buildings. "And don't you ever let me catch you trying to sneak in here again, you hear?"

"I hear." Erich finally managed a couple of words, which made the man named Andy laugh.

"You probably understand every word we've been saying, huh?"

"Not every word." Erich shook his head as he hurried out the gate, rubbing his arm where he'd been squeezed by the first guy. But Andy called after him.

"Hey, wait a minute."

Erich didn't wait.

"You like Hershey bars?" asked Andy.

Erich froze but wasn't sure if he should turn around. It was a trick. Had to be.

"Hershey's?" the man repeated. "You know, chocolate?"

That did it. Erich looked over his shoulder, just to be sure. The tall man reached out, offering a brown-wrapped candy bar. Erich couldn't ever remember having a Hershey bar all to himself. A bite, once. Never a whole bar. His stomach danced at the thought.

"Come on," said Andy. "Take it before I change my mind. You've got to be hungry, right?"

Erich could already taste the chocolate, sweet and warm and rich. He turned back to accept the gift, expecting the man to pull it away at the last second. But no.

"*Dankeschön.*" Erich looked up at the man whose skin seemed as dark as the chocolate he offered. "Thank you."

"Andy!" someone yelled from inside the *flughafen*. "Need you back here!"

"See you around." The man winked at him as he turned to go. "Only next time, you stay outside the fence, okay?"

"Andy!" The voice did not belong to a patient man.

"Aren't you going to eat it, kid?" Andy asked as he started back through the main gate. "I thought everybody liked chocolate."

"Ja." Erich fingered the treasure, knowing how wonderful it would taste. It had been given to him, had it not? Didn't he have every right to enjoy it? He paused. "Yes. But it will be for … Oma, Grandmother."

And before he could change his mind, he slipped the precious Hershey bar into his shirt pocket, turned, and sprinted away.

2

KAPITEL ZWEI

GOOD EXCUSE

"I told you, I didn't steal it." Erich pedaled up Potsdamerstrasse, Potsdamer Street, as fast as his old bike would let him. "I can't believe you would even *think* that of me."

"Sure." Katarina checked over her shoulder and slowed down as they entered the spooky wasteland of the Tiergarten—once a beautiful, green city park but now sheared of all its trees by bombs and firewood scavengers. Some of the grand statues still stood, headless, high on their columns, ruling over rubble and ruins. Others had long since toppled to the gravel pathway. "But I don't think your story's going to help us explain what took us so long to get home."

"We'll just tell them the truth. A big green lizard monster grabbed me and wouldn't let me go. I was ... kidnapped!"

Katarina wasn't buying it.

"Okay, then how about a big American soldier in a brown uniform?"

"And then are you going to explain why he stopped you?"

"Well—"

Katarina led the way on a rusty old bike with warped wheels and a chain that fell off every other block. Which was actually fine, since it gave them a chance to catch their breath. Meanwhile, Erich did his best to keep up on Frankenbike, a monster he'd wired together from the skeletons of several dead or smashed bicycles he'd discovered in bombed-out buildings. At least traffic seemed lighter now, after dinner, so that was good. Shops had closed for the day. But his front tire—the one that didn't fit quite right—wiggled a little more than it had earlier that evening, and he had to keep jiggling the handlebars to keep it lined up right.

"You going to make it?" she asked him. They had skirted the Soviet sector of the city, districts to the east where Russian soldiers were in charge. Here at the eastern edge of the American sector, jeeps with American soldiers—like the ones at Tempelhof—passed them every couple of blocks. The cousins would reach Oma Poldi Becker's flat in a minute or two.

"Yeah, I'll make it. It's just this stupid wheel." He gave it one more good shake, jerking back his handlebars and planting the wheel squarely on the pavement. That should fix it.

And it did—sort of. The next thing he knew the front wheel bounced out ahead of him, even as he continued to pedal. Without a front wheel, the front end of his bike nosed down and jammed the fork into the street, launching him chin-first to land—OOMPHH!—spread-eagle on the pavement. The frame of the bicycle tied itself into knots around his legs, bending him into an impossible pretzel.

"Erich!" Katarina kneeled next to him, but her words only buzzed in his ears. "What happened?"

What happened? He slowly untangled himself from the bike and tried to sit up straight.

"Wheel decided to go solo, is all." And sure enough, it still bounded down Bernauerstrasse. "It wanted a new life as a unicycle."

"Quit being silly."

"Who, me? I'm all right." By that time he'd collected himself enough to stand up. That seemed to be a good sign: all his arms and legs worked. His elbow and right knee looked a little scraped. The worst part: his jaw.

That, and the warm red stain on his shirt.

"No, you're not." Katarina pointed at his chin and wrinkled her nose. "Oooh, gross. You're bleeding all over the place."

Nicht so gut. Not so good. He cupped his chin in his hand, trying to keep from making more of a mess all over everything. That helped a little, but he had broken open his chin more than just a little. Good thing they were only a half-block from Oma Poldi's place.

"Can you walk?" Katarina wanted to know.

He nodded, still cupping his chin tightly. And he supposed they looked a bit odd, him holding his chin and dragging what was left of Frankenbike, her juggling his runaway front wheel while pushing her bike.

"Don't make a big deal out of it," he told her. "It's just a little scrape."

Or not. Five minutes later their Oma Poldi dabbed carefully at his chin with a damp washcloth and told him it most certainly was *not* just a scrape. Katarina turned green and looked the other way.

"Does that hurt?" Oma studied him with her sharp blue eyes. Everything else in her body had wrinkled or twisted: her face and her hands, for instance. Her knees, she said, from spending so much time on them, praying. Her cheeks had aged even more in the last few years, like prunes that had been left out in the pantry too long. And at times she coughed so hard and so long that Erich and Katarina thought she might never be able to take another breath. Just a little tickle, she told them, but Erich's mother had called it chronic bronchitis, which sounded a lot more serious than just a tickle.

But she had nursed her share of children and grandchildren back to health, patched plenty of skinned knees and broken arms. She caught her breath and repeated the question.

"No, Oma." He shook his head and winced. Not as long as he didn't move or breathe or try to open his mouth. Otherwise, no problem.

"Then what were you doing out on the street at this time of night?" Of course she wanted to know everything as she patched up the gash on his chin with a slice of medical tape, cut into careful little pieces, just like a doctor would have done. And maybe she wouldn't tell her daughter-in-law, Erich's mother. Or maybe she would. But her question reminded him of something, and he reached down into his shirt pocket.

"I went to get you this." He presented the prize—a little broken, a little squashed, but all there. And for just a moment her eyes widened, the same way Katarina's had.

"Where did you get that?" she asked him, but she had to know the answer. Only the Americans—

"A soldier gave it to me." Erich still held the Hershey bar out to her, hoping the wrapper had stayed clean. "He was as dark as the candy. You should have seen him."

"He *gave* it to you?" She raised a knowing eyebrow and looked over at Katarina just to be sure. Katarina nodded.

"Take it, Oma." He held it out. "When was the last time you had chocolate?"

For a moment she let herself gaze out her apartment's single window, with her view of the tall steeple of the once-beautiful *Versöhnungskirche,* the Reconciliation Church, not much more than a block away.

"When your father was still—" she began, and her voice trailed off. Even she could not say the word *alive.* "Well, he would work on his sermons, and on his way home Saturday afternoon, a half bar of chocolate for his old mother he would bring."

It hurt Erich to smile as she shook her head and came back to the here and now.

"But that was before you were born, of course. Before the war … and all this."

All this. A city in ruins, where most of the men were dead or disappeared, and where women worked all day shoveling rubble and clearing collapsed buildings, bucketful by bucketful. *Rubblewomen,* they called them. Like Erich's and Katarina's mothers.

"Then you should have it, Oma." He held it out once more. She wasn't making it easy. "Please."

"On one condition only." She finally held out her hand, then took the chocolate and divided it into three parts. "That you kids will share it with me."

Of course there was no arguing with Oma Poldi, and no way to get her to nibble more than a couple of squares of the rich chocolate. Erich closed his eyes and let it roll over his tongue, again and again, before he finally had to swallow. And when he opened his eyes again they watched the Russian soldiers on the street below. One of the thick-armed guards had stopped a row of people as they stepped off the S-Bahn streetcar. He rummaged through their shopping bags and removed what he wanted: a loaf of bread, several packages of cigarettes, a kilo of coffee. They meekly took back their empty shopping bags, stared at their shoes, and hurried off.

Is this what his father had meant by "blessed are the meek, for they shall inherit the earth"? Well, there wasn't much left to inherit, not in this Berlin. Only what the Soviet soldiers could steal from people coming in from the other side of town, the western side. And, as the Soviet blockade wore on, that supply was getting thinner and thinner.

Just like Oma Poldi.

In this section of Berlin they kept starving old women alive with hand-me-down bars of American chocolate, smuggled across the invisible line between east and west.

"It's not getting any better, Oma." Katarina was the first to break their silence. "Why don't you come live with us, over in the American sector?"

Oma carefully licked her fingers, making sure to get every chocolate smudge. She seemed to think about her grand-daughter's question for a moment before answering.

"How could I leave?" She stared out the window once more. "You know my grandfather grew up in this building. Your father and uncle, even. I belong in this place where God has called me."

And there could be no arguing with that, chocolate or no chocolate.

"And besides," she added, "your father and his brother loved the people in this neighborhood. Some of them are still left here. Frau Schnitzler. Poor Ursula Ohlendorf. They all went to church at the *Versöhnungskirche*."

The church, the *kirche* that now lay quiet and empty and ruined.

Just like Oma Poldi. She could hardly speak anymore. Still she kept Erich in her sights.

"They all heard your father preach against the Nazis, against the evil. I honor my sons by staying, now. So this is my place. This is where I will live and die."

"Oma." Erich nearly choked on his last bite of chocolate. "You're not going to—"

But he knew she *was* going to, even if he brought her a chocolate bar each day. She needed much more than snacks to survive.

"Of course I am going to die, when God wills it." She reached out and mussed his hair, and the effort must have drained her. She leaned back in her chair and closed her sunken eyes. "Now go on home. You're a sweet boy to be bringing your old grandmother sweet treats, even if you're a bit clumsy on that old bicycle of yours."

He'd almost forgotten about the accident and his blood-stained shirt. He still had some explaining to do at home.

"I'll be sure to let your mother know that you were visiting here," added Oma. "And a bit late it was."

Erich rose and nodded, reached over and kissed his grandmother on the cheek.

"Let's go, Katarina." And he was out the door before his cousin, bounding down the stairs two at a time. "I'm headed back to the airport."

"What are you talking about?" Katarina stepped on his heel as they hurried through the landing to the door out to Rheinsbergerstrasse.

"Tomorrow, that's what I'm talking about. I'm going to try again."

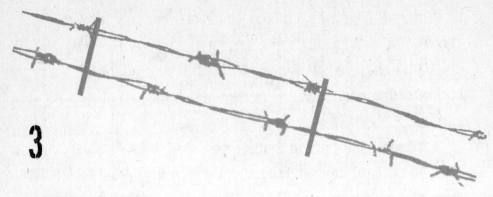

3

KAPITEL DREI

ERICH BECKER'S PRIVATE WAR

"Yes, Erich, I'm glad you were visiting your grandmother yesterday." Erich's mother barely got the words out as she sat at the small kitchen table the next evening, her head in her hands. "Sitting there in that dark apartment all alone. Almost starving, and goodness knows the Russians don't care what happens to old people in that sector, much less if they get anything to eat."

It was true. Erich licked the back of his spoon to make sure he'd cleaned up his serving of thin cabbage soup, though it didn't begin to put a dent in his stomach-clutching hunger. The kind of hunger that just ate and ate at him, that sapped his energy and made him want to just stay in bed all day. Come to think of it, though, maybe it was a good thing they'd had soup tonight; it had taken little effort to chew. His jaw still hurt when he bit down, but no one needed to know. He touched the bandage on his chin and looked up at his mother, who had closed her eyes.

Was it just his imagination, or did his mother look almost as old and wrinkled as his grandmother? No blood relation, of course; Oma was his father's mother. But since the Americans had killed his father in the war, it seemed his mother had aged a whole generation, maybe ten years for every one.

Her hands had been the first to go: cracked and bleeding, covered now with calluses and blisters from holding her shovel. Her nails had nearly disappeared, too. But who could stay young-looking while shoveling bricks and rubble all day, clearing the city of ruined buildings?

It was, she told him, the only job she could find. And though it paid nothing, it helped them get extra ration cards, so that was good. But at what price? And who had dropped the bombs that had destroyed all those buildings in the first place?

She never wanted to talk about whose fault it was, or who had killed Father. Sometimes in the middle of the night, though, he heard her crying. And now, with her eyes closed, she moved her lips as if answering all his questions.

Why did they drop so many bombs on us, then divide our city?

Where will we find our next meal?

How long will Oma live?

Finally her lips stopped moving. The dull hunger still gripped him, still made him dizzy and sleepy and angry all at once. Of course they'd prayed for help; how could they not?

And if crying or screaming would have helped, he would have done that too. But not today.

Their single stub of candle flickered and sputtered, and still his mother didn't move, only held her chin and let her long dusty hair flow freely. *Good for her*, Erich thought. *She's sleeping.* He licked his fingers and quietly tried to snuff the flame—*fsst!*

"Ow!" he muttered; the feeble little flame fluttered back to life. "I thought I knew how to do that trick."

Brigitte Becker blinked and shook her head in the half-dark, as if waking from a dream.

"Oh!" She straightened up and checked her hair. "I must have dozed off."

"That's okay. Thanks for breakfast."

"Mm-hm." She nodded and began to push out her chair, and yes, he'd said *breakfast*. It took only a few seconds for her to freeze, though. "Wait a minute. It's not … Oh, you!"

She smiled for the first time all evening, a shy grin that spread slowly across her tired face. And that was the best reward of all.

"Erich Becker, you're more like your father every day. He would do the same thing to me. Tell me the silliest lies with a straight face, then when I believed him, he would grin and—" She paused, dishes in hand.

"Mom, I don't remember him very well anymore." Six years ago felt like a lifetime. "I can't even remember his face, except for the pictures we have. I'm sorry."

She set down her dishes by the sink and rested her hands on his shoulders for a moment.

"Don't be sorry. You were much younger. It was a long time ago."

"I do remember the last time I saw him, when I took his lunch to him at his study at the church." He paused. "Do you remember the last thing he said to you?"

His mother's face went serious again. She turned to the small window over the sink that revealed the narrow space between their apartment building and the next one.

"I don't know why I asked that," he told her. "It just slipped—"

"He was talking about books, always talking about his books." She bent down to the bowl in the sink, splashed water on her face. The candle made her shadow dance on the wall, weird and larger than life.

"What kind of books?" he finally asked.

"Luther. He told me he'd been reading a volume of sermons by Luther. That he very much liked it."

"Doesn't every Lutheran pastor read Luther?"

"I suppose." She nodded, hugging the dish towel to her chest, remembering. "But this was different. He said that if anything ever happened to him, I should not forget a book called *Dr. Martin Luther's Sämtliche Schriften*."

"*Collected Writings*?" In other words, a book of sermons and short essays. "That was his favorite?"

"I think so." She dabbed at the corner of her eye with the towel. "He said he would explain it to me, but he had something urgent he had to do at the church first. So I still don't know what he was talking about. It didn't come up for another couple of days; we were so busy. And then the air raid—"

Erich knew the rest of the story, the bombs that fell near the church, how they never found his father's body, all that. But not the part she'd just told him.

"You never told me that before. That part about the book."

"It's the first time I've thought about it in years, Erich." Finally she turned back to face him. "I never thought it was important to anyone else. Now, as I was saying before I dozed off, I do appreciate your visiting your grandmother. But you must be more careful on that old bicycle thing of yours."

"Just a loose nut holding the wheel. I fixed it fine."

"Maybe, but your chin is not fixed so easily, and the stain in your shirt didn't come out all the way."

"You don't need to worry about me, Mom."

"I still don't like the idea of you wandering all over the city. It's not safe these days."

"Safer than before. I was thinking of going to see Oma again tonight."

She started to say something, then nodded quietly, took a half-cup of flour, and poured it carefully into a handker-chief-sized piece of clean brown wrapping paper she'd saved. Everything was saved, used again and again. She folded up the corners and tied it off with a loop of string, also saved.

"Then, my good pastor's son, you will take this to her, as well."

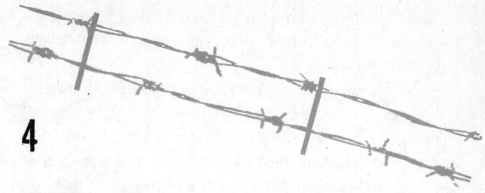

4

KAPITEL VIER

UNDER THE FENCE

"But it says 'No Trespassing,' Erich." Naturally Katarina would feel the need to remind him. Cautious Katarina. She ran her finger along the big block lettering in the early evening shadows. The sign was wired crookedly to the eight-foot chain-link fence, just below the coil of barbed wire. "By order of—"

"I can read English as well as you can, Katarina." He found a hiding place for his bike behind a tombstone, good enough for a few minutes until he got back. Through the fence and across the runways he could make out the glow of floodlights at Tempelhof Airport, where twenty-four-hour crews unloaded emergency supplies from American and British cargo planes. Around them, the city circled the airport, forcing pilots to come in low and slow over bombed-out neighborhoods.

"Well, I think we should just turn around and go home, before we get in trouble and it starts pouring rain. This place is creepy."

"Yeah, the monsters and the spies are watching us, huh?"

Everyone knew about the spies. Men who watched everything the Americans did and reported it all to the Russians, in exchange for a few ration cards. Men who counted the planes taking off and landing, and probably a lot more than that besides.

"You just make it into a joke, Erich. But it's not—" Katarina started to leave as a jeep carrying two American soldiers bumped toward them across the huge expanse of landing strip on the other side of the fence.

"Down!" he hissed and pulled her behind a taller tombstone. Without warning, they tumbled blindly into an open pit.

"Oh!" Katarina scrambled to her knees. The jeep whined past them, its headlights casting long shadows across the graveyard for a brief moment.

"Bomb crater," Erich decided. Good thing for them no one had yet repaired this end of the St. Thomas Kirchof, the St. Thomas Cemetery. He hadn't seen it before, even in the daytime when he'd come to scout the place out. This would make a good hiding hole, though it seemed a bit weird, considering where they were. He realized he'd have to move fast before another patrol came by.

"You sure you won't come with me?" He rolled out of the waist-deep crater and crept over to the fence. This *was* the fencepost, if he remembered right. He yanked at a corner of the chain-link wire where it attached to the metal pole. No luck. Had someone fixed the loose piece of fence? He moved on to the next one. It had to be here.

"Seriously, Erich, I still don't think this is a good idea."

He would expect her to say that. Meanwhile, he found the right spot and peeled the corner of the chain link back a couple of feet. He looked up at her and pulled the little package of flour from his shirt pocket, the one his mother had wrapped.

"You think this half-cup of flour is going to do Oma any good?" Erich held up the package.

"That's not the point."

"It isn't?" Erich felt the back of his neck redden. "Why don't you tell me the point?"

She crossed her arms before answering. "I don't think this is about trying to survive, Erich. I think it's about ... trying to get even. You want to do whatever you can to get back at the Americans. This is the private war of Erich Becker."

"That's crazy." Erich crossed his arms to match hers. *"Wahnsinn."*

But why did she always have to be so under-his-skin right?

"Look, Erich. We both know we have to do something to help Oma. But this isn't the way."

"You said that before. But I'm not just going to sit around waiting for her to starve to death while we figure out plan B. Is that what you want?"

"That's a dumb question. I just can't go along with your plan this time."

Erich sighed and ran a hand through his light, short-cropped hair.

"Look, I'm sorry, but I don't know what else to do. So I guess you can come with me, or not. I think I have it figured out this time, but I could still use your help."

She looked at him and swallowed hard, but finally pressed her lips together and shook her head no.

"You may think you have it figured out, Erich, but that doesn't make it right."

"Fine." He tossed the little package at her and turned back to the fence. "If you could just deliver this for me, I'd appreciate it. Tell Oma I'm coming back with a crate of Hershey bars."

That's right. And maybe no one else had noticed this loose piece of fencing; it wasn't quite big enough for an adult to skinny through. But an underfed German kid like him?

He ducked as another big American cargo plane took off. He felt his chest rumble as the huge bird gathered speed and roared east over the bombed-out apartment buildings, shaking any glass windows left in the Neuköln neighborhood. The supply planes left Berlin every three minutes, as regular as a good Bavarian cuckoo clock. He couldn't help smiling—before he remembered his mission.

No! He gritted his teeth and reminded himself how much he hated the men who flew those planes. The same men who had dropped the bombs. The same bombs that had killed his father. The same father who had always promised that God would protect them.

And then he didn't smile anymore.

Instead, he took a deep breath and held it, looked up the runway and back. All clear.

"Hold it open, please," he told her. "I'm going in."

"No, Erich." She crossed her arms. "I can't help you steal."

"Come on, Katarina. You make it sound like I'm some kind of criminal."

Her shoulders fell when she sighed.

"You're not a criminal, Erich. But you don't need to do this."

"And if I don't, we line up for our one lousy loaf of bread for five people, and Oma gets skinnier and skinnier. If the Americans hadn't—"

"Don't start blaming the Americans for our problems again."

"But can't you see what fakes they are? First they try to kill us all, and now ... now they think they're our new best friends, just because they toss a few cigarettes to the beggars on the street corners. You ever tried to eat a cigarette?"

Katarina made a face. "They're the ones bringing the food, Erich. They didn't have to do that."

Erich smacked his forehead with the palm of his hand.

"Don't you get it, Katarina? They're still the enemy. They will always be the enemy. And when they're the enemy, the old rules don't work."

"But for how long, Erich? And we're supposed to love our—"

"Don't preach at me. Besides, it doesn't matter. You're too worried about the rules, when we need to be worried about helping Oma."

"Okay, but that doesn't mean you can just sneak in there and steal whatever you want. What about everybody else in Berlin who's hungry? Can you look me in the eye and tell me this is the right thing to do?"

Erich closed his eyes and rubbed his forehead.

"I don't know if it's the right thing or not. I only know that I have to try."

"We'll get the food some other way." She wasn't giving up so easily. "My mother gets some more ration cards in a few days. We can share, the way we've been doing. If they catch you—"

"Nobody is going to catch me."

Yeah, but if he didn't hurry over to the supply planes, he'd lose his chance.

And his nerve. So he would crawl under this fence, with Katarina's help or not. He flattened himself out like a worm, poked his head under the chain link ... and the wire caught like a trapdoor, square on his back.

"Ow!" Great. Now he couldn't move forward, couldn't back up, couldn't quite reach back. The wire had skewered him pretty well. "Katarina! I'm stuck. The wire's digging into my back. You have to—"

He didn't have to finish; she lifted the corner of fencing so it unhooked from his shirt.

"Thanks." He wriggled through the rest of the way on his belly. Getting his only shirt dirty didn't matter. He dusted off and straightened up on the other side.

"I'll be right back."

"I still don't think—"

He didn't let her finish. Instead, he hunched low and sprinted along the edge of the fence. As long as the jeep patrol didn't come back too soon.

"Can I have your bike if you don't make it?" she called after him.

"Sure. Sell it for a thousand *reichsmarks.*" He grinned. There's the old Katarina. "You'll be rich."

But he almost tripped over his own feet when he glanced back one last time. In the distance, just behind the *kirchof,* he noticed a light flicker in the window of one of the apartments. Nothing unusual about that, only—

"What?" Katarina must have seen the look on Erich's face, and she turned to see for herself. Too late, of course.

But before the light went out, Erich was sure he saw the shadow of a man bringing a pair of binoculars to his eyes. Even in the dark there was no mistaking.

Someone was watching them.

5

KAPITEL FÜNF

CORNERED

Don't breathe … Erich blended into the shadow behind the
American transport plane, waiting for just the right moment as
the pair of American mechanics strolled by, their heels clicking
on the tarmac. One told a mumble-mumble joke, and the other
laughed.

Erich waited.

But this time he knew who to look for, when to look for them,
and where the floodlights would betray him. Mechanics hurried
by as the planes came rumbling in, right on time, while flight
crews and unloading crews scurried from plane to plane. He
was pretty sure even Andy, the friendly black American with the
chocolate, would not be very happy to see him again so soon.

"Ready to roll again in twenty minutes?" one of the flight
crew asked his pilot. The two men paused in front of a truck,
barely three feet from where Erich hid.

"Yeah, if we can get the ground crew to get the lead out. This one's full of food."

This one was called the *Berlin Baby*, a name painted on the side by some soldier-artist who had included a funny picture of a diapered baby with wings on his back and coal smudges on his face. Hadn't he seen this one before?

But Erich didn't have time to admire the artwork; he knew he would only have a matter of seconds before the unloaders arrived. So as the men moved away he slipped under the plane and clambered up the rope ladder, as if he belonged there.

Slip in, borrow some groceries, slip out.

But he paused in the airplane's doorway as Katarina's words echoed in his mind.

You may think you have it figured out, Erich, but that still doesn't make it right.

Oh, brother. He gripped the side of the door, trying to take the next step, but he couldn't get his feet to move or his hands to stop shaking. What? And out of nowhere a thought popped into his head.

What would Dad have thought of Erich the Thief?

He knew the answer and sighed. After all these years, the conscience he thought had died with his father ... well, maybe it hadn't died all the way. It wasn't because he was scared, but—

"I can't do this," he whispered, and for an unguarded moment he rapped the inside of the dark airplane with his fist.

But that didn't help. And it didn't help that a jeep was heading right for his plane. Too late! He dived into the plane's belly and out of sight behind a dark pile of crates, wondering what he was going to do now. This wasn't the plan.

Even worse, another worker must have found his way to the plane, right on Erich's heels. Give me a break! Once more Erich held his breath; he was getting pretty good at that. He heard a grunt as someone hauled up inside the plane, then a shuffling sound as the worker came nearer.

"Erich?" came a voice. "Erich, I know you're in here."

Erich blinked back the surprise. Katarina?

"Shh! Back here!" He tried to signal her deeper inside, but he wasn't sure she could see him in the dark.

"Back where?" She stumbled toward him just as the engines turned over and fired to life.

What in the world?

"This one's done, guys." An American bellowed from just outside the door as the engines revved. Americans seemed to do that extremely well. Bellow. Erich had no problem hearing the orders: "Button it up and get on out of here."

What had happened to all the food the men had been talking about outside?

"Wait a minute!" Katarina turned to the door, but Erich caught her wrist just in time and pulled her down to his hiding place.

"We're dead if they find us in here," he shouted into her ear over the roar of the engines.

"We're dead if they don't," she shouted back. "We have to—"

"Hold still for a minute." His mind raced. "We'll think of another way."

Meanwhile, another American shoved a large wooden crate through the double doors and hopped aboard. He pulled the doors shut behind him and threw a strap around the crate before hurrying through the near-empty cargo hold to the forward compartment. The food flight must have been some other plane. Erich held a hand over his cousin's mouth, just in case she had any ideas of calling for help. Maybe they could get back to the door before they took off.

"Whoa! Hang on," he told her. The plane jerked forward as engines revved and they started down the runway. And instead of nearly reaching the door, Erich tumbled and slid through the empty hold, a bowling ball flung down the alley.

"Easy for you to say." Katarina joined him as they tumbled into a heap in the tail section. But by that time they couldn't have bailed out of the plane even if they'd wanted to. All they could do was steady themselves as the plane gained speed, turned, gained even more speed. And it must have been enough for the crate to work itself loose and tumble against the inside of the plane. A moment later he could hear it sliding back to crush them.

"Your legs!" It was the only thing Erich could think of. "Stop it with your legs!"

So they both sat in the tail of the American plane, legs out, waiting for the crushing blow that never came. Instead, the plane lifted off and banked left. The box must have hung up on something halfway back through the plane.

"Let's just keep an eye on it." Erich sat ready to catch the loose cargo with his shock-absorber stance. So did Katarina.

"How did you ever find me here anyway?" he wondered.

"You weren't hard to follow. I thought maybe you needed somebody to keep you out of trouble."

Erich might have laughed if they hadn't been in so deep. Sneaking onto an American cargo plane? Bad enough. Flying off in one? He wondered what the soldiers would do to them when they finally landed at the other air base, or when he and Katarina were found out. It would be nothing compared to what his mother would do to him when he got home.

If he got home.

Right now, though, they had to deal with the Americans. One of them appeared at the door to the cargo hold a few minutes later, probably looking to see what had fallen. He pulled a dark blue baseball cap a little lower over his forehead and carefully made his way toward the back of the plane, gripping handhold loops as he did.

"I thought we tied this stuff down!" he yelled back at the open door. Erich couldn't tell how many others there were—probably at least two flying the plane—but they had already lit a couple of dim overhead lights in the main cargo hold. *Nicht so gut.* Not so good. Katarina looked over at him, and neither of them said a word.

"A wonder we didn't lose these crates through the back end when we took off." The airman talked over his shoulder as if the others could hear him, which they most likely couldn't. From a few feet away Erich could barely make out the man's words.

In any case, the soldier's eyes followed the pile of boxes, still half-secured, back to the loose box snagged on a side door handle, and finally farther back to the two young Berliners huddled in the shadows. Okay, here it came. For a moment Erich thought the guy might jump out of his skin.

"Lieutenant!" He never took his eyes off the kids. "You're not going to believe this. I think we've got us a couple of passengers."

6

KAPITEL SECHS

THE DEAL

"You want to explain to me what you two are doing aboard this airplane?" the pilot growled, and Erich knew that no jokes were allowed here. A younger co-pilot studied them from the right seat, while the man who had discovered them stood guarding the cockpit door, arms crossed.

Not that they had anywhere to run.

"It was—" Erich wanted to be sure he used the right English words. It was one thing to listen to the Americans and British speak, quite another to speak for himself.

"It was all a mistake." Katarina finished the sentence for him. "I was looking for Erich. He is my cousin. We were getting off the airplane, but the plane started moving. We didn't know what to do. We didn't mean to be on the airplane when it took off."

Which was a pretty good try, Erich thought.

"Yeah, I can see how a person might get confused between a C-54 and the S-Bahn tram downtown." The co-pilot pulled a checklist from behind his seat, as if this sort of thing happened every day. "Can't you, Lieutenant?"

"Humph." The lieutenant wasn't smiling yet, just gripping his steering wheel and staring straight ahead. "Still doesn't explain what you kids were doing on the plane in the first place."

"I was hungry," Erich blurted out. What did they have to lose by telling the truth? The pilot raised his eyebrows as he went on. "And my oma, she is not well. She has not a good ration card, so we must bring her extra food. She has to eat, or she'll die."

"Her and a million other Berliners," the pilot snapped. "So you thought you could just push your way to the front of the chow line, huh?"

"Easy, Lieutenant." The co-pilot acted like a referee in a soccer match. "He's just a kid. Don't you have a son back home?"

Erich was still trying to figure out what "chow line" meant. But finally the pilot's scowl eased up a bit.

"Yeah, about their age." He glanced over at Erich. "What are you, kid, fourteen?"

"*Dreizehn.*" Erich knew the English number; he just wanted to be sure. "Sirteen."

Or "thirteen," if you stuck your tongue out at the "th" sound the way the Americans did. They studied each other for a long moment, the pilot and the stowaway. And still Erich wondered how they would get out of this one.

"By the way, I'm Sergeant Fletcher." The smaller, round-faced man in the right seat nodded at the long-faced pilot. "Lieutenant Anderson's the serious guy in the pilot's seat, and Wilson there is in charge of the maps."

The other men barely nodded as Erich and Katarina introduced themselves.

"Did you fly bombers also?" Erich had to know. Maybe his chin stuck out a bit at the question, maybe it didn't. But the co-pilot whistled.

"Whoa, Lieutenant. I think I know where he's going with this."

The pilot nodded and checked the sky ahead, and Erich noticed the muscles on the back of the man's neck tighten.

"What are you trying to do, Erich?" Katarina whispered to him in German, obviously so the men wouldn't understand. "Have them throw us out of the plane without a parachute?"

Erich stood his ground.

"Er, he likes airplanes." Katarina gulped and tried to explain. "I think maybe he just meant—"

"I know what he meant," the pilot interrupted. His eyes narrowed as he turned back to the challenge. "And yeah, kid. If you really want to know, I flew sixteen missions over Europe. Don't think anybody likes the way it turned out, and I'm sorry about that. Is that what you were thinking? You think I liked dropping bombs?"

When Erich bit his lip and nodded, the pilot turned back to his instruments, mumbling something about Krauts and their lousy war that wouldn't end.

"Gotta admit, I like this duty a lot better," the co-pilot put in, sounding much more cheery than he probably needed to. "Not as many people shooting at us, and the natives are a little friendlier ... well, most of the time."

"Yeah." The pilot kept his gaze steady. "Piece of cake. All we have to do is stay right in the middle of a twenty-mile corridor between Rhein-Main base and Tempelhof, hold at exactly 170 miles an hour, exactly six thousand feet, exactly three minutes behind the last bird and three minutes in front of the next one. And all to feed a bunch of Krauts."

"He's a real nice guy," said the co-pilot with a wink, "once you get to know him. But you two. Anybody back home that's going to be worried about you?"

Erich crossed his arms and said nothing as Sergeant Fletcher asked them question after question, the way a policeman would. Where they lived. Their mothers' names. Where they went to school.

"Stop answering his questions," Erich told Katarina, but she wouldn't listen. The co-pilot wrote it all down on his clipboard.

"I have a feeling your mothers aren't going to be too pleased to hear you stowed away on an Air Force plane," Fletcher told them, scribbling yet another note. "And by the way, you know what the U.S. government does to stowaways?"

Erich stiffened. But they didn't have a chance to ask before the pilot broke in.

"Hold on, Rhein-Main. How close?" The lieutenant pressed the earphone against his head a little tighter and leaned to check out the front windshield.

"What's up?" asked the co-pilot, snapping to attention and pulling up his own earphones.

"Rhein-Main tower says there's an unidentified aircraft coming right at us, four o'clock."

The words had hardly left the pilot's mouth when a gray streak fell out of the sky, cutting right across their nose. Katarina shrieked and Erich gasped, but the two men hardly flinched.

"Yeah, we see him," the lieutenant spoke into his microphone. "Saw him, I mean. Russki fighter shaved a few of our wing feathers off, is all. Thanks for the warning."

Erich was still trying to catch his breath. Kill him now, or kill him later, what difference did it make? Sergeant Fletcher hadn't finished what he'd started to say about what they did to stowaways.

"Oh, and by the way, tower," the pilot added, "we have a couple of visitors with us that you're going to want to know about—"

Erich looked at Katarina and wished she hadn't followed him to the airport, wished she hadn't said anything to the Americans. Now they knew everything. What kind of trouble waited for them on the ground?

"I'm Sergeant Fred DeWitt." A fresh-faced man in a sharply pressed brown uniform greeted them as they climbed down from the Skymaster to the wet pavement below. "Hold it right there."

Erich grabbed his cousin's arm and braced himself. So this was it. But instead—

"No, no," said the man, whose toothy grin was slightly crooked. "Relax. Here, look at the camera, and don't grit your teeth like that. Smile."

Smile? Is this what they did to all their condemned prisoners? Shoot their pictures before they carted them off to prison?

Pop! The dark-haired man's camera caught them with its flash as they huddled next to the plane, trying to stay dry in the drizzle. But smile, he would not. *Nein.*

"Furchtbares Wetter heute, nicht?" the man with the camera asked them in flawless German. Well, *that* got Erich's attention in a hurry, and yes, it *was* horrible weather today, as the man said. Even Katarina stopped shivering to take a closer look.

Some kind of trick?

"Das tut mir leid," he told them. "I'm sorry. I didn't mean to scare you. I just thought they told you everything."

"There's no telling him nothing, DeWitt." Sergeant Fletcher landed on the pavement beside them. "He's a hard one. And I get the impression he's not all that keen on Americans."

"Thanks for the tip, Sergeant." DeWitt gave the other man a friendly half-salute. "I think I'll be able to handle it."

"Good luck." The co-pilot glanced up at the darkening sky and wiped a sudden splatter of cold rain from his face. "Lieutenant Anderson and I didn't get very far with him. But hey, come to think of it, you speak the lingo pretty good, don't you?"

Their host shrugged as a truck approached to load them back up. The co-pilot stepped aside.

"Well, so long, kids. Hope you find your way back to where you belong."

Katarina nodded politely, but Erich couldn't bring himself to wave at Sergeant Fletcher as he trotted off. Okay, he'd acted friendly. But that meant nothing. And Erich still couldn't just forget who these people were, or what they had done. Katarina looked at him out of the corner of her eye but said nothing. By this time, though, Sergeant DeWitt looked ready to go too.

"Will we be able to go back to Berlin?" Katarina asked, looking back up at the plane. DeWitt laughed, though the question didn't seem funny at all.

"Sure we'll get you back. I've just been assigned to take care of you while you're here in Frankfurt. We haven't been able to contact your families yet, but we're sending a messenger to your homes in Berlin. And we have a plan to get you home."

So that was what all the questions on the plane were about, Erich thought.

"By the way, you ought to be thanking me for getting you out of hot water. Brass was going to send MPs to get you when word got out. I talked them into letting me handle this for a PR project."

Hot water? Brass? MPs? PR? Up to now, Erich thought he'd understood most of what the Americans were saying.

"You are a soldier?" Katarina looked at him with a questioning expression.

"Oh, right." He looked down at the bulky box camera hanging from a strap around his neck. "Guess I'd be wondering too. I'm a reporter with the *Stars and Stripes* newspaper. So yeah, I'm a soldier. Maybe not like some of these other fellows. Came in through the reserves, never saw combat. They found out I had a bad back. So they gave me this camera and told me to go out and write news stories, if you can believe that. I studied history at college, so I guess they thought, *Here's a college boy—*"

He paused for a moment and gave them a sheepish grin, as if he'd suddenly realized he'd been talking too much.

"Das tut mir leid," he told them once more. "I'm sorry. That's probably a whole lot more than you want to know."

Erich still said nothing. What else could they do but follow this man through the drizzle to his car? He seemed about the same age as their mothers.

"Anyway," he told them, "long story short, I've been looking all over for a great human-interest angle for this whole airlift thing, a way to put some real faces on the operation. A good

PR angle. Public relations. You know, making sure everybody out there understands what we're doing. So when I got the call from Ops tonight, I knew we had something. You're perfect."

They both looked at him with a blank "huh?" expression.

"Unless you wanted to spend some time with the MPs? You know, military police?"

"Oh, no." Katarina raised her hand.

"I don't think so," Erich agreed.

"That's what I thought you'd say." DeWitt grinned as he reached for the door handle of a gray military sedan. Katarina took the backseat; Erich the front, though he kept his arms crossed. "So I'll take you back to Berlin myself, but we're going to be taking a lot of pictures and asking a lot of questions. Fair trade?"

No trade. Erich knew he couldn't trust this man. But he had to know—

"How did you learn German so well?" he asked. Because this was way more than just "Guten Morgen, Frau Schmidt" (Good morning, Mrs. Schmidt) or "Wie geht es Ihnen?" (How are you?). The man's accent didn't make him sound like a Berliner, but he could have passed for a Bavarian, easy.

"Oh, right." DeWitt started up the car and put it in gear. "I was raised by my grandparents in Cleveland, Ohio. Thing is, they both came from Munich, so they never spoke a word of English to me."

This was getting a little more interesting.

"So I guess you could say I was raised German," continued DeWitt, "which sure comes in handy over here, but it caused me all kinds of grief back home in the States."

"What kind of grief?" Katarina wanted to know, then brought a hand to her mouth, as if she'd asked too much.

"Hey, wait a minute." DeWitt's easy smile spread across his face once more. "I thought I was the reporter around here. Why don't you let me ask *you* a few questions this time?"

So as they drove through the dark streets of Frankfurt, he asked them about their home and about their life in Berlin. And Katarina gave him the happy version, the one without the hunger pains and the war, without the nightmares and the bombing, without the ugly things they somehow survived but wished every day they'd never known. Erich knew it was much better to tell those kinds of stories—rather than the gritty, real ones—like it was better not to pull off a scab before the wound had healed.

A few minutes later they pulled up to a three-story apartment building, windshield wipers still keeping time.

"You'll be staying here tonight," DeWitt told them. "In my apartment."

"Not an army prison?" Erich wondered, but of course not. DeWitt didn't even carry a gun.

"No, the base doesn't have enough beds right now. Barracks are all full. Although if you'd prefer, I could probably find you a small German jail to sleep in."

Erich shook his head, but the soldier with the camera wasn't finished.

"Listen, I know it's been hard," he told them. "I have relatives over here too, you know. Pretty distant, but my grandparents told me all about them. So if you ever want to tell me your *real* story, I'd be glad to listen. But I understand why you told me what you did."

So he knows what really happened. Without another word, Erich followed his cousin out of the car, back into the rain. And he wondered what else this man might know, this American who was also a German.

7

KAPITEL SIEBEN

THE STORY

Erich stopped at the door to the apartment. It had once been very nice, with fine wood trim and fancy stained-glass windows. The apartment even shared a bathroom down the hall with four or five other tenants. Imagine that, indoor plumbing! Now the gray and the dust had taken over, just as it had back in Berlin. Someone had tried to sweep the stairs, but even so the plaster ceiling still rained war dust on everything.

"You are not married?" Katarina asked when they'd climbed the stairs to the sergeant's apartment. One look could have given her the answer. Not messy, exactly, just a little like … a bachelor's apartment.

"*Nein.*" He folded his hat carefully and set it down on the front table. "No."

At least he was neat. But his apartment held only a typewriter on a rickety card table, several piles of papers, an empty kitchen, a small bedroom filled by a single bed, and a lumpy faded couch in the front room. The only decoration he seemed to own was a small framed photo of two stern-looking older people, hanging crooked just above the couch. Erich guessed it might be the Bavarian grandparents. Oh, and on the couch lay a German Bible, dog-eared and obviously well read. Erich figured this was another trick to make them think the American could be trusted.

"So here's the deal," DeWitt told them, opening a tiny coat closet and pulling down clean towels for them. "The *fräulein* will sleep in the bedroom. I have a clean sheet for you. The men will sleep out here. Breakfast is at oh-seven-thirty tomorrow on the base, so make sure you're ready to go by seven fifteen. We'll take a few more PR photos there after breakfast, maybe of you guys standing next to the airplanes, and then catch a flight into Berlin by oh-nine-hundred. That means we land at Tempelhof by eleven thirty. A few more pictures that afternoon around the city, and we'll have you back home safe and sound in plenty of time for dinner. Any questions?"

They both shook their heads no as he grabbed a toothbrush from a glass on a shelf and started for the door. The bathroom, Erich remembered, was shared by the entire floor.

"Sorry I don't have any extra toothbrushes for you. Wasn't expecting this kind of company." He paused and pointed at the couch. "You're welcome to read my Bible while you're waiting, though."

With that he popped into the hallway, leaving them in the strange room in a strange city, wondering how this had happened to them.

"This is all my fault." Erich paced the floor just in front of the closed door. "I shouldn't have let you come."

"It wasn't your decision." Katarina ran her hand across the German Bible. "And besides, I couldn't leave you to fly here by yourself, could I?"

"No, but it was kind of—" He didn't dare use the word *fun.* "Well, I mean, did you ever think you were going to get to ride in one of those planes, ever in your life?"

"Never. But I wonder what our moms are thinking right now."

Erich had been wondering the same thing. "I hope they get the message soon."

"That's not going to keep us from being in huge trouble."

"You're right about that," said their host as he reappeared at the door. "But we'd all better get to bed now. Tomorrow's going to be interesting."

Or *crazy,* perhaps, like this entire adventure was crazy. *Wahnsinn,* insane, like the chase dream Erich had later that night, after everyone had fallen asleep. The men chasing him had no faces, only guns and parachutes, and it was just like the dreams he'd had ever since the war that never seemed to end had started, only in this dream the soldier who finally landed on his head was an American, like—

"Wake up!"

Someone grabbed his shoulder and shook him awake. Erich could only cry out and punch at his attacker. He connected with something hard: a cheekbone, maybe. But the enemy only grabbed him by the wrists and held him. So this is how the torture would begin, but not without a fight.

"Erich!" the man's voice hissed at him in the dark. "Settle down, kid. *Ruhig!*"

Erich couldn't think of too many reasons to settle down, but finally he realized where he was. It was still pitch dark, and a door creaked open behind him.

"Erich?" Katarina asked in a small, sleepy voice. "What's going on out there?"

The neighbors must have heard everything too.

"Herr DeWitt?" An older woman's voice came through the hallway door. "Mr. DeWitt? Is everything all right in there? I heard screaming."

"Everything's fine, Frau von Kostka. I apologize for my guest. He's just having a bad dream."

"Ah, *ja*. It sounded like a battle, and your guest, he was losing."

"I'll bring you a couple of extra potatoes tomorrow, Frau von Kostka. *Gute nacht.* Good night."

"Knowing that will help me sleep better—as long as there are no more battles."

They heard Frau von Kostka shuffling back down the hall as she returned to her apartment. Katarina closed her door again too. And Erich sank his head back into the arm of the couch as DeWitt returned to his pile of blankets on the floor.

"Do we have a truce, kid?"

No truce. Erich pressed his lips together. *But—*

"I'm sorry I hit you," he finally managed. "You're not going to write about this in your newspaper, are you?"

"That depends on how much you pay me."

Erich wasn't quite sure if the guy was kidding, not at this hour. Midnight? Three a.m.? Outside he heard a plane take off in the distance. They weren't very far from the air base.

"Sorry, kid. Just trying to make a joke."

Erich didn't answer as he stared up at the dark ceiling. And it sounded like Fred DeWitt wasn't done asking questions yet.

"I know there haven't been a lot of things to joke about in Berlin lately. Did you have to leave the city during the war?"

Erich thought about not answering, about pretending he'd gone back to sleep. But he had to tell the American something.

"Thanks to you, we did. We were almost killed too."

"I'm sorry to hear that. What about your father? Was he—"

Erich spit out his answer to the dark, which was somehow easier than face-to-face.

"My father was drafted into the army when I was seven. My older sister was nine."

"He was in the *Wehrmacht*, the army?"

Erich paused before deciding to answer.

"A chaplain. He never shot a gun in his life. But just before he had to leave, he went back to the church where he was a pastor, I think to bring home a few things. Then your bombs started dropping. He never made it back." No one said anything for another long minute. DeWitt finally cleared his throat, though, and his voice sounded far away.

"I'm very sorry to hear that."

That's what they all said. But Erich wasn't through yet.

"They told us we had to leave, my mother and sister and I. The bombs were coming day and night, all the time. The city wasn't safe. But you know that part of the story."

Fred DeWitt didn't answer.

"My oma was supposed to leave too, but she was too stubborn. Always stubborn. My mom nearly went crazy about it. We have no idea how Oma survived all the bombs, except that none fell on her building. She always talks about angels."

Still no answer from DeWitt.

"But they took us to a little village a hundred miles north, to get away from American bombs."

Erich made sure he reminded DeWitt the bombs were *American*.

"Is that where you stayed the rest of the war?"

"*Nein.* A few months before it all ended, the government took us away once more, except this time we had to travel in cattle cars, which was horrible because we all got lice from the old straw we had to sleep in."

"I've never had lice."

"It's like torture; they bite you all over. And you get these big welts. But that wasn't all. We stayed in a farmer's barn for a couple of months, and then we nearly froze to death, until my mother decided we should go back to Berlin."

Erich took a deep breath, and it truly seemed like someone else was telling the story, not him. He only felt numb now, nothing else, and he didn't care who was listening. The tears had all been cried, the feelings all felt, and the only thing left was the dull anger. But still he went on.

"So we walked all night and all day, and the roads were full of people who had the same idea we did. Everybody just wanted to get home, no matter what. We could die out there, or we could die back home. Except we didn't know we were walking straight into the Russian battle zone. During the day the Russian planes came flying over, shooting their machine guns at us. We had to dive into the ditches, only some of us didn't—"

His words caught, and he took a deep breath. His voice fell to a whisper, even softer than before.

"—some of us didn't make it. A man that we knew, a milkman from back home in Berlin, he helped my mother and me bury my sister."

There. Was that the kind of story the American had expected? But now Erich had to keep going.

"So we stayed in an abandoned castle for a couple of days, stayed there with only the servants. But there was nothing to eat so we had to keep walking, ten or fifteen miles a day. I had to carry our suitcase, until we found a baby carriage we could use. The baby had died. Don't know why we didn't too."

"And the Russians?" DeWitt found his voice again.

"The Russians came almost every day, just stopped us and pointed their guns at us, took whatever they wanted. What did we have left? Some of those guys had watches all the way up their arms."

"Pirates. But you finally made it home."

"What was left of it, after the Russians—well, we had to hide for a month until the Americans and the British and the French came. But my mom says we were lucky to find another place to stay in. Our old house was a pile of bricks."

"Look, I know I keep saying this, but I'm really sorry."

But Erich didn't say anything else. Couldn't. He just lay with his eyes open in the dark, listening to the planes taking off and landing, fighting back the sleep and the dreams of the men and the parachutes, chasing him, chasing him—

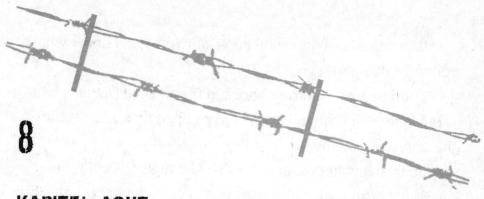

8

KAPITEL ACHT

JUST AN ACCIDENT

"Would you look at that shiner!" Fred DeWitt bent in front of his shaving mirror, squinting at himself.

Erich stretched and pulled the covers back over his head, wondering if he'd really told all his stories in the dark, or if it had been a dream.

Probably a dream. And what was a "shiner," anyway? He peeked out between his hands.

Oh. Now he remembered, and the knuckles on his right hand seemed a bit sore to match.

"You see that?" DeWitt turned toward him and pointed to the dark purple halo of a bruise around his eye. "I haven't had a black eye like that since I was a kid. Good thing it's not going to be me in those pictures."

Erich kept an eye on the man shaving as he slipped on his clothes.

"You're not mad?"

"Who, me?" DeWitt chuckled. "Nah. You didn't know what you were doing. Did you?"

"Coming out!" Katarina knocked from inside DeWitt's bedroom before she came out, but she stopped for a moment in the doorway, staring.

"See what your cousin did to me last night?" DeWitt balanced his army cap on his head and slicked down his hair. "I should have put him to bed with boxing gloves."

"It was an accident," Erich mumbled as he followed DeWitt out the door. Katarina still gave him a funny look, as if she weren't sure she should believe him. But they hardly had time to talk about anything as they followed the sergeant to breakfast.

Erich wasn't sure why DeWitt called it a "mess" hall, since the floors looked clean enough to eat from, and he might have called it a dining hall. But the noise, and the men, and the food!

"Extra big helping of scrambled eggs for my friends here, Sam." DeWitt pointed them out to a large black man standing behind a long counter crammed end-to-end with steaming stainless-steel platters of scrambled eggs, sausages, toast, and a kind of porridge. Erich wasn't quite sure what to do when DeWitt pulled his plate and tray in closer and the cook dished up a huge helping of everything.

"You sure you can handle all that, kid?" asked the cook.

Erich checked his plate, now piled high with breakfast, and he almost grinned. Almost.

"I can handle it."

So could Katarina, for that matter, who put away nearly as much as her cousin, thank you, *dankeshön*. And they were almost through their fourth piece of toast with butter and orange marmalade when DeWitt looked at his watch and scooted back his chair.

"Sorry to cut things short, kids." He wiped his mouth with a napkin. "But we have some snapshots to take and a plane to catch."

Well, that was fine, but Erich still had eggs on his plate. He shoveled as much as he could into the next few bites. If only he could take home even a piece of toast—

"Jussaminute." He held up his hand for them to wait, gasped for air, and felt some of the eggs go down the wrong pipe.

Nicht so gut.

"Ahh-HAACK!" As Katarina pounded him on the back, he couldn't help turning his head to the side and spraying out the half-chewed eggs—

—right on top of a pair of shiny black military shoes.

And no, he really did not want to look up and see whose uniform he had just decorated. Better to slide under the table now. But as he caught his breath he had no choice.

"Er … Captain Matthews." DeWitt sounded a little edgy. "These are the German kids I told you about. The ones we're doing a story on."

Erich finally gathered the courage to look up at a frowning man in uniform, who looked down at his egg-speckled shoes.

"And we're terribly sorry about that, sir." DeWitt held out a napkin. "But actually, we're a little late, and we'd probably better get going."

DeWitt grabbed Erich's arm as he apologized once more, and they scooted out of the mess hall.

"Don't we have to take our trays back to the kitchen," wondered Katarina, "like everybody else?"

"Not now," mumbled DeWitt. "Just follow me."

They walked over to the airfield, where they spent the next half hour standing beside air crews, saying "Cheese."

"He's just making me more hungry," whispered Erich, "talking about cheese all the time." And Katarina scolded him when he pulled three big packages of Juicy Fruit chewing gum from his pocket.

"Where did you get that?" she asked as they waited for DeWitt to talk to a pilot about their ride back to Berlin.

"Those guys over there gave it to me when we were taking all those pictures. Said I looked as if I could use it. Do I look that desperate to you?"

"Not so much today. Today you just look full. Did you get enough eggs back there? Enough to eat?"

Actually, yes, today he felt full, for the first time in . . . well, a long time. He looked down at the candy in his hands but stuffed it back into his pocket again when he noticed someone watching them from outside the airfield's chain-link fence.

"What are they looking at?" he wondered aloud. But he knew without asking. And it wasn't just one or two kids now, but three, five, ten of them.

All staring. He tried not to return the stare, tried to ignore the little question that chewed at the back of his mind, the question that swirled in the pit of his stomach and made him want to shrink.

"Almost makes me feel guilty."

Katarina looked at him with a crinkled nose, as if she didn't understand.

"Do you have a fever, Erich Becker?" She reached over and felt his forehead with the palm of her hand, the way a mother would do. "You've never talked about feeling guilty before."

He felt his pockets to make sure the gum was still there. Oh, and the Hershey wrapper from the candy bar he'd eaten himself. At least he had another one to bring home with him, for Oma, the way he had promised. But—

"But I ate all that breakfast," he answered. "That was more than we have in a whole week back home. For sure a whole lot more than what Oma gets. Didn't that cross your mind?"

"Of course it did."

Still, he couldn't keep from staring back at the crowd of kids on the other side of the fence. Meanwhile, DeWitt motioned them over to a plane near the middle of the lineup.

"Here's our ride," he told them as the last coal-smudged worker came out of the hold, slapping the dust off his hands. "All loaded and ready to fly."

As they stepped closer, a little door in the belly of the plane opened, then shut again with a snap. Not a door, exactly; more like a mail slot.

"What's that?" Katarina wondered aloud.

"Pre-flight," answered DeWitt. "They're just checking everything to make sure it works. That's the flare chute, for dropping out emergency flares."

Erich wasn't sure he liked that word, *emergency*. Hopefully they wouldn't need anything like that. But as he climbed inside the plane, he looked back toward the fence one more time, and he felt the gum in his pocket.

And he started to get an idea.

"Well, if it isn't our friendly local stowaways!" Sergeant Fletcher came out to greet them in the crowded cargo hold. It was stuffed to the gills with bulging burlap sacks. He grinned and slapped Erich on the back. "Ready to head back home?"

"Just a few more photos." DeWitt explained what they'd been doing as they took their places behind Lieutenant Anderson, who grunted and nodded at them as he went through his pre-flight check. Fletcher didn't seem to notice his grumpy pilot.

"Did you see that horrible mess?" He pointed with his thumb at the back of the plane. "I thought we were doing just fine carrying flour and powdered milk. But somebody got the bright idea to fill us up with sacks of coal. My clean airplane!"

The lieutenant kept flipping switches but paused a moment to catch his co-pilot's attention.

"Pre-flight checklist, Fletcher."

"Right, sir!" Fletcher grabbed his trusty checklist as they worked, flipping switches and pulling knobs, adjusting levers, checking and rechecking each step. The pilot would bark things like "Bypass valve down!" (whatever that meant), and the co-pilot would echo every word. Erich watched, though he did take a moment to poke at the flare chute just behind the pilot's seat. His idea could work.

Ten minutes later the four engines finally roared to life, each one in turn, sending storms of smoke swirling behind them. Throttle up. All four engines spun up to full power as the plane lurched and bumped through puddles on its way to the head of the takeoff line, then forward faster faster faster, until they nosed up and left the muddy airfield below.

"Think you'd ever like to fly a plane like this someday?" DeWitt asked Erich above the roar of the engines a few minutes later. Erich nodded before he could catch himself. Well, what did it matter? He looked over at the bundles of parachutes tucked under a seat. He couldn't do this by himself.

"Do you have any handkerchiefs, DeWitt?" Erich pulled the gum from his pocket, and the American gave him a puzzled look. "All we need are a few handkerchiefs and some string."

By the time they approached Tempelhof Airport, Erich and Katarina held three handkerchief parachutes ready, each one tied with string at its four corners and each one carrying a pack of Juicy Fruit.

"Hold one of the chutes up for me." DeWitt aimed his camera at Katarina, and the flash went off. "Perfect. In fact, this whole idea is perfect. Don't know why I didn't think of it myself. This is going to be front-page."

"I didn't mean for it to be on your front page," mumbled Erich. Maybe he'd made a mistake.

"Just don't get in my way," growled their pilot as they once again neared the city.

"You're sure the chutes won't just land on the roofs of one of those ruined apartment buildings?" Fletcher wanted to know.

"Kids will find them," Katarina told him. "Especially over the Russian sector. They watch the planes."

"The Russian sector?" Lieutenant Anderson frowned. "Nobody said anything about the Russian sector. We drop stuff over there, and we're going to stir up a hornet's nest of trouble."

"Oh, come on, Lieutenant." DeWitt folded the parachute back up and carefully wound the string around it before handing it back to Katarina. "It's just candy. What can it hurt?"

"I'm telling you, it's a bad idea."

Erich bit his lip, wondering if the lieutenant might be right. What *would* the Russians do if they saw little parachutes coming down on their territory? But by that time DeWitt was grinning and snapping photos nonstop as Anderson and Fletcher worked to bring the plane in low and slow over the city. The lieutenant called for their before-landing checklist, and Fletcher knew the drill.

"Heater switches off," barked the pilot.

"Off."

"Main tanks on."

"On."

And so a little lower, even lower than the tops of some of the crumbled apartment buildings. Katarina, who knew the Russian sector as well as anyone, served as spotter. She chose Fletcher's window and gave them a running review of the city below.

"Wait a minute, Katarina." Erich watched the roofs below and felt his stomach turn flip-flops. "We'd better not do this."

"Too late," she told him. "We're coming up on the Tiergarten! And oh, there's the Brandenburg Gate! We're going so fast. The *Versöhnungskirche* is coming up. I see the steeple, near Oma's apartment. That would be a good place. Is the little door open?"

DeWitt pried open the little door and *whoosh!* Even at landing speeds, the wind rushed by the plane outside. And for a moment Erich panicked as he thought of what it must have been like for the men who dropped bombs over this same city, not so long ago.

"It's fine." DeWitt didn't look worried. He just held one of the gum parachutes ready and looked up. Katarina held up her hand and counted down from three.

"*Drei, zwei, eins … now!*"

"Chutes away!" Erich and the American stuffed the three bundles out, one after the other, and Erich wondered how much trouble they would be getting into because of this silly idea, or who would find the treats. One of the hungry kids on Rheinsbergerstrasse, probably. DeWitt whooped, then straightened up when Lieutenant Anderson shot a glance over his shoulder.

"Done yet?" asked the pilot. "I don't want those things snagging my landing gear or nothing."

"No snags," answered DeWitt. "But that won't be the last time we do this."

"No kidding?" Fletcher glanced out the window, and DeWitt pointed at him.

"Absolutely positively. You, my friend, are going to help us with the biggest gum drop in history."

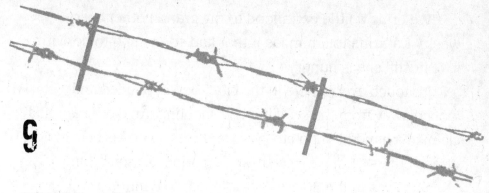

9

KAPITEL NEUN

FIRST MEETING

"You've never been in a taxi before, have you?" DeWitt grinned at them in the back of the car.

Was it that obvious? Erich tried not to look so stiff as he watched Urbanstrasse go by. Imagine! Riding in a taxi for a walk home that would take only twenty minutes, at the most! He wondered what the kids in the neighborhood would think when they saw him and Katarina with the American soldier.

"My father took a taxi, before—" Katarina's voice faded, and it reminded Erich he wasn't the only one who had lost family during the war. Outside their window, though, it looked as if the war had never ended. On the corner a half dozen street people nearly mobbed a man as he set out a garbage can with restaurant food scraps. The grin left DeWitt's face.

"We bring a little extra food to my grandmother every week," Katarina told him, as if that had something to do with it. "But still she is hungry."

"It's tough everywhere in the city." DeWitt nodded and looked away from the scuffling and shouting. An older man had claimed a handful of potato peels and was doing his best to fight off the others. "But we'll see if we can bring her something."

"She lives in the Soviet sector," Erich told him.

"Oh." The man's face fell even more. "That's not good."

"We've tried to talk her into leaving." Erich thought it never hurt to ask. "Maybe she would listen to you."

"Wish I could help you." DeWitt shook his head slowly. "But there's really nothing I can do. I can't even cross the line, the way you kids can."

Maybe true. Still, it seemed as if the American should do *something* to help Oma.

"This it?" DeWitt looked out at the battered apartment building. And no wonder he asked. The building next door had been hit by a bomb during the war, taking it from four stories down to one and a half. Much of the outside wall between the two had crumbled as well, taking with it most of Frau Landwehr's living room on the third floor of their building and forcing the *frau* to find another place to live. The rest of their building seemed to sway in the wind, and only half the windows had survived. Herr Eickmeyer on the fourth floor had a great view of Tempelhof from his open patio (which had, before the bombings, been his kitchen).

"Second floor," Erich announced as he jumped from the taxi. "Follow me."

Katarina paused by the curb for a moment. "Want me to come along?"

"Maybe that's a good idea." Erich looked up at their window too. "My mom won't kill me if you're there."

"We did our best to explain to your mothers," DeWitt told them as he bounded up the short flight of front stairs. "But I can't guarantee anything."

Except that he would be charming and funny and make it sound like a grand adventure—in perfect German, which of course led to the story about growing up with his German grandparents in Cleveland, Ohio. Erich's mother listened to his story, wide-eyed, and then apologized many times for not having any coffee to serve her American guest.

"I'm so sorry, but I traded our last ration for bread, and—"

"I understand." He twisted his hat in his hands as he sat on their most comfortable living room chair, the one with the stuffing escaping the sides. "And now I hope you'll understand about your children. I mean, about your son and your niece. They were only trying to find food for their grandmother."

"Yes, I know." Frau Becker lowered her eyes. "We pray for her every day, but—"

"Erich told me about her." He nodded and looked as if he understood, while Erich's mother glanced up once, blushed, and returned her gaze to the worn rug. "And I want you to know that I appreciate kids who care the way they do."

She nodded as he went on.

"Although next time they go flying with us, we'll want to make arrangements first."

This time it was Erich's and Katarina's turn to stare at the rug.

"I'm very sorry they put you through all this trouble." Erich's mother was still apologizing.

"Not at all." He shook his head. "As it turns out, my editor is pretty excited about all this. We have some incredible photos so far, and the wire services are already picking up the story. Erich and Katarina are going to be in papers all over the world."

"This is what I sent you to do?" Frau Becker looked at her son sideways, but the twinkle in her eyes told Erich he was probably safe. Hopefully Katarina still had the measure of flour for Oma, as well.

"But only if it's all right with you," DeWitt told her. "I want to be sure we have your permission."

"Of course." Frau Becker smiled.

"And I want you to have this." DeWitt held out a bulging cloth sack. "Just to thank you for letting me work with the kids."

"Oh, my goodness!" Frau Becker's eyes lit up even more as she pulled out cans of Spam, condensed milk, and peaches.

"Just a few things from the commissary that you probably can't get around here lately. Maybe you can share them with your mother-in-law."

Frau Becker hid her face in her hands and cried, which only seemed to confuse the American.

"I didn't mean to upset you, Frau Becker. I just—"

"You're very kind," she interrupted him. "It's just that I haven't seen this kind of food for so, so long."

And it didn't seem so strange, then, when she laughed softly over the food, the kind of laugh that says, "I can't believe this is happening to me," and asks, "Am I dreaming this, really?"

But Erich enjoyed the sound; in fact, he couldn't remember the last time he'd heard his mother laugh. For sure before Father had died. And he knew just how she felt as he quietly lifted the peaches, to be sure he wasn't just seeing things. Real American peaches, packed in syrup from Oregon, United States of America. He tried not to drool. After so many months of eating hard bread crusts, he wasn't quite sure how to deal with all this food, this real food. Just as he wasn't quite sure how to deal with this American.

Because, wait a minute—the man had to want something. They all did, and as DeWitt talked about his German grandparents again the thought came crashing back on Erich like a door slamming in his face. Of course. No one gave away food for free, just because. Erich could have kicked himself for letting down his guard, for believing it, for not seeing the strings attached.

"Look, I have a three-day pass for this assignment," DeWitt said as he rose to his feet and fitted his hat to his head. "If it's all right with you, I'd like to see if we can get some more pictures of the kids and the gum drops, maybe from the ground this time, if we can get some other planes to do the drops too—"

"Gum drops?" Erich's mother didn't quite follow.

"Oh, I'm sorry." DeWitt chuckled. "I didn't tell you about that."

And as Katarina told the story of the candy parachutes, Erich backed away slowly, trying his best not to get caught in the web his mother had stepped into. Surely he'd made a mistake helping this DeWitt. Even Katarina looked as if she'd let down her guard, lured on by all the food. Who wouldn't be? But Erich wanted to shout: "Don't you see? This man isn't what you think he is! He's an American, and you can't trust people who bomb us one day and pretend to be our friends the next!"

But nothing would come out of his mouth, so he just slipped to the edge of the room with his arms crossed and his mind racing. There had to be a way out of this trap. Meanwhile, DeWitt told them he'd be back the next afternoon at three, flying over with more gum, and would the Reconciliation Church still be a good place to drop them?

10

KAPITEL ZEHN

HEAD-TO-HEAD

"Well, he's not my aunt's *friend,* exactly." Katarina did her best to backtrack, but the next afternoon the kids in their oma's neighborhood weren't buying it. "He's just an American newspaperman, and he's doing a story on the gum drop. That's what we're helping him with. That's all."

"You're helping an American?" An older boy named Wolfgang scowled at them with his big hands on his hips, then looked around at the group of kids who had gathered. Though he stood a head taller than most of them, he hadn't ever really been a bully before—just a pain. Now he acted like both. "Did everybody hear that? Katarina and Erich are working for an American soldier!"

"I'm not," Erich said as he crossed his arms, but no one heard.

How else were they supposed to answer? Erich didn't forget where they were; in the Soviet sector of Berlin, you had to be very careful what you said on the streets. People disappeared here, taken away by Russian soldiers, who always snarled and grunted. Sometimes the people never came back.

And they'd heard stories too. They'd seen the Watchers in the windows, like the one who had been tracking them with binoculars when Erich slipped into the airport. For all they knew, Wolfgang was feeding the Russians information too.

"It's just for a newspaper. Just some pictures." Erich tried to make it sound like no big deal, but so far it wasn't working.

"Then where did you get all the food, if he's not your mom's *ami*?"

Wolfgang leaned on the last word, *ami,* and everybody knew about *amis*. The American boyfriends who visited the homes of the women who had lost men during the war. The soldiers who came to visit with food, or cigarettes, or sometimes fancy clothes.

"Katarina told you he's not my mom's *ami.*" Erich stood up to Wolfgang and clenched his fists. No one had the right to talk about his mother like that. She hadn't done anything wrong.

"Prove it." Wolfgang stood where he was and kept the mocking grin pasted on his face.

"We don't have to prove anything to you." Katarina wasn't backing down either, bless her heart. This bigmouth was talking about her aunt, after all. "All you have to do is stand right here in the *strasse* while the American planes fly over, only don't get run over, of course, and in about fifteen minutes you'll see."

They hoped. DeWitt had promised he would be on the flight from Rhein-Main arriving right at three o'clock, hadn't he? And while Erich didn't trust the American's word for a minute, now probably wasn't the best time to say so.

"I'll see *what*?" Wolfgang laughed. "Is your mom's *ami* going to wave at us as he flies by?"

"You'll see." Katarina sounded more sure of herself than a girl had a right to be.

"Humph." Wolfgang still wasn't convinced, but so what? "He's going to have to do something pretty special, because in a few days the capitalists are going to be leaving the city with their tails between their legs."

"What's a capitalist?" asked a little blonde girl named Ilse.

"He means everybody but the Russians," explained Katarina.

"But that's stupid." Erich kept his arms crossed as he looked straight at Wolfgang. "Who told you that?"

"My teacher. We're going to be learning Russian too. Pretty soon it'll be the world's language. Is your mom's *ami* teaching you English?"

Erich might have hit him then; Wolfgang deserved it. But Katarina pulled him back by the shoulder, and his hands flew up for balance.

"It's not worth it, Erich." Katarina was probably only trying to help. Trying to keep him from getting into trouble. Trying to help him turn the other cheek, the way it said in the Bible.

But either Wolfgang hadn't read that verse or he didn't care. Because a moment later he tackled Erich and they tangled on the street, arms and legs flying. Katarina was there too, yelping and elbowing her way into the middle of the fight, while all the other kids gathered around and chanted, *"Am-i, am-i, am-i!"*

Or something just as brainless. It all just sounded like a roar in Erich's ears as the blood pumped in his head and he tried to stay alive. His chin throbbed with pain all over again. And he felt a punch connect to his ribs, then another. He heard the larger boy's grunt, felt Wolfgang's hot breath and forearm choking him. But the strange thing was that once Wolfgang had tackled him, all the hot, angry feelings dribbled away. Erich only wanted to keep from being choked to death.

"Am-i! Am-i!"

What was wrong with those kids? They cheered as if they were watching a soccer championship, only this match was over as quickly as it had started. Erich felt the lashes of the cane, saw Wolfgang roll away and scramble to his feet before running off with his crowd of squealing rats. Then Erich heard the scolding voice of his oma over everything, as in, "What in the *world* is going on here?" and "What are you thinking, attacking my grandchildren? Hoodlums! Go home!"

She helped Erich to his feet with a firm grip on his ear. Katarina saw the kind of help he was getting and jumped up without any help, thank you. Then he had to explain what happened as Oma herded them back to her apartment.

"No grandchildren of mine are going to behave like this."

"But—"

"Is that what you want people to know you for? For street fighting?"

"No, Oma, but—"

Finally back in her apartment, she settled into her easy chair as if the effort had taken more than she had to give. And it had. She dropped her cane to the floor in front of her and coughed long and hard, so long and hard that Erich thought about running to fetch a doctor. Her face turned blue, and her hands shook as if she had been the one beat up, not Erich.

"And this — ," Oma finally managed, sort of catching her breath. "This is the kind of Christian example you want to set? They'll know you are a believer because of the way you use your fists?"

"No, Oma." Erich patted her on the back; what else could he do? "But he said Mom had an *ami*."

Their grandmother stiffened at his words and looked over at him, her eyes barely open but now blazing and alive. "Oh, so he said that, did he? Well, then I hope you gave him a good poke in the nose."

With that she closed her eyes and rested her head back against her pillow. But her breaths sounded even more short and shallow, rattling and deathly. Erich straightened his shirt and looked over at Katarina. The look on her face told him she knew too. It was going to take a whole lot more than Fred DeWitt's food to help their Oma Poldi survive the summer.

As they thought of Fred DeWitt, the rattling windows told them an American plane had come in low once again, winging over the city toward its touchdown at Tempelhof. Erich and Katarina couldn't help looking out the window, staring at the dozens of little white parachutes that blossomed in the sky over their city.

"He's really doing it." Erich's jaw dropped open, and he counted ten, fifteen, no, at least thirty little parachutes. Most drifted directly down onto Rheinsbergerstrasse, where they'd been fighting just a few minutes earlier. Well, yes, this *was* where they'd told him to drop them, but—

"Did you think he wouldn't?" Katarina glanced back to check on their now-sleeping grandmother.

"How should I know?" Erich just shrugged. But as they watched, he had no doubt what was happening below them. A handful of the neighborhood kids jostled and jumped to catch the parachutes as they drifted to the street. Who had ever seen anything like this before? The kids giggled and laughed at the candy rain of chocolate and gum and other sweets—until an ugly snub-nosed Soviet army truck came flying around the corner. One little girl barely made it to safety as the truck screeched to a stop in the middle of the street and two soldiers jumped out.

"Hey!" Erich almost leaned out the window to shout, then thought better of it. "Those soldiers need to get their own candy."

But the men shooed the kids away like flies and scooped up as much of the treasure as they could. The good thing was that some of it had fallen out of reach onto a nearby rooftop, and some had disappeared into a pile of rubble. A couple of parachutes even got hung up high in the bell tower of the *Versöhnungskirche*.

Still, the blank-faced soldiers managed to corral most of the booty. Some they tossed into the front seat of their jeep; some they held up to the light of the sun to study a little more carefully. Well, sure, it might look like a candy bar, and it might taste like a candy bar, but it could still be an American trick. A nuclear bomb shaped like a piece of gum, perhaps? And even if it wasn't, no telling what would happen to these children if they were allowed to eat a few sweets, especially when they were starving to death.

"Look at Ilse." Katarina giggled and pointed at the little girl on her knees, peeking around the truck. "She's trying to grab a piece before it's all—"

Erich saw her. Too bad one of the soldiers did as well. He stomped on the candy chute with his big black boot before poor Ilse could quite reach it.

"Hey." Erich groaned, but of course they couldn't have helped her, even if they'd been down on the street. They could only watch as the soldiers picked up the last few candy chutes, barked at the kids to clear the street, and then roared away in a cloud of thick black smoke. No doubt the Soviets would pro-test this to the American military leaders very soon.

Finally the smoke cleared. Kids came out from their hiding places once more, careful at first, then dancing and hollering and waving their prizes like trophies of war. The soldiers hadn't been quick enough to grab everything.

"Look what the *ami* dropped for us!" yelled a little guy named Rolf, skipping in circles and holding out his parachute. He popped the gum into his mouth and started chewing as if his life depended on it. "Katarina was right! *She was right!*"

So she was. Ilse had grabbed a piece of chocolate and started skipping around with the rest of them, waving her prize in the air. She stopped once in a while to smell it and hold it up, studying it almost as the Soviet soldiers had.

Only one of the kids wasn't dancing. Wolfgang just stood in the middle of the dance, staring up at Erich and Katarina with his hands on his hips as if it were all their fault that such a wonderful, horrible thing had happened on Rheinsbergerstrasse. Shouldn't they be sorry for bringing this capitalist candy down on everyone's heads? Erich couldn't help feeling a chill creep up his spine before the other boy finally turned and marched down the *strasse,* looking very much like a soldier himself.

KAPITEL ELF

LUTHER'S KEY

"This is wonderful to have you all here, so wonderful," Oma said, looking at her family the next Sunday. Her eyes glittered with tears, and her voice trembled when she spoke, as if the words might shatter before they reached the ears of the people sitting around her little kitchen table. They'd walked over together after church. Oma had set out her only lace tablecloth and a small tapered candle she'd saved for a special occasion. She had chairs for herself and the two mothers, wooden boxes for Erich and Katarina, and a sturdy pile of books for Katarina's seven-year-old sister, Ingrid. It didn't matter that they knocked elbows or that the chairs teetered dangerously. As Oma said, "Ein gemütlich abend ist." And a festive evening it was. Especially with all the food they had brought with them, most of it hidden under their clothes to avoid attracting the attention of soldiers on the street. Yes, a feast!

"A whole can of American Spam meat," Oma wheezed, "and those berries—"

"Cranberries," Erich's mother told her, picking up the can from its place of honor on the table. "It's something they grow in America. The sergeant said it is festival food in his country, for their special giving thanks dinner."

"*Cran*-berries." When Oma said the word it sounded more like *krrrahn-behr*, and they all had to laugh. The problem was, that only set off Oma's coughing once more.

"Have you been to the doctor again, Oma?" Katarina's mother asked. Concern wrinkled her round face. She tried to offer a glass of water, but Oma only shook her head no.

"They tell me there is nothing to do about it, but to go home and die." Oma plucked the handkerchief from the pocket of her apron and breathed through it like a mask. "The young Russian medic even told me to try not to breathe, since that would only make it worse. Ha! Do you think he was serious?"

Even as sick as she was, she could still tell a joke on herself. But Erich's mother wasn't laughing.

"I'm serious, Oma," Erich's Aunt Gerta said. "The doctors we have over in the American sector are much better. A little medicine could help."

"Maybe it would. Maybe it wouldn't."

Erich knew his aunt could say nothing else to her mother-in-law. They didn't want to get into *that* argument again, about leaving this house or this neighborhood. And they would not argue about being friends with the American soldiers, either, not unless they wanted to upset Oma, make her start coughing again.

"So tell me," Oma began, managing to change the subject. "This DeWitt, he is your friend?"

Erich couldn't remember seeing his mother turn so red before.

"I don't think we could call him a *friend* exactly, Oma."

That's for sure, thought Erich, taking a bite of meat and rolling it around in his mouth.

"I don't want you to think wrongly of me," Erich's mother whispered.

"Wrongly?" Oma shook her head and rested her hand on her daughter-in-law's shoulder. "You've cared for your family through all this time, and now you've come back to care for me. You will do the right thing once more. Just like Ruth."

Ruth from the Bible. Naomi had lost her husband and two sons, but her daughter-in-law, Ruth, stayed by her, even when she didn't have to. Come to think of it, maybe his mother really *was* like that. But when the subject changed to serious stuff like ration cards and food lines, Erich decided it was time to let the adults talk. After clearing their dishes, he and Katarina headed outside.

"You remember that story too?" Katarina asked as she and Erich tripped down the *strasse* toward the church.

"You mean about Naomi and Ruth? I'm a pastor's kid, re-member?" And that made him think of something his mother had talked about once, something he'd been meaning to do.

He told Katarina his plan and looked up at the *Versöhnungs-kirche* bell tower, just around the corner on Ackerstrasse.

"Are you sure you want to go this way?" Katarina asked.

This way would lead them right past Wolfgang's house.

"He's just the neighborhood watchdog." Erich tried not to notice the eyes that watched them go by. "I don't understand why he cares so much about where everybody goes."

Katarina shrugged her shoulders. She didn't seem to mind as much as he did.

"Maybe he's training to be a Russian spy."

They both laughed, while Erich looked back once more to make sure Wolfgang hadn't followed them.

But getting away from Wolfgang wasn't the hard part.

The hard part was actually making their way through the church building, once they'd pushed open a splintered door, past piles of bricks and chunks of stone.

"Wait a minute." Erich paused for a moment at the back of the sanctuary, where the late-afternoon light spilled in from above. Even more filtered down around the bell tower, where he could see two of the gum drop parachutes, tangled in the spire.

No one had yet cleared the rubble from this part of the church. Snow and rain from the last few years hadn't made things any better. It was going to take a lot of work to make this a place where people would come to worship again.

A lot of work. Gaping holes reminded Erich of the beautiful stained-glass windows he'd loved to stare at, back when he was little.

"Erich, I'm totally confused. Do you remember where your father's study—"

They both jumped when something fluttered just over their heads, but Erich had to laugh.

"Just a couple of pigeons."

They watched a pair of birds circle once inside the sanctuary before they found the hole in the roof and disappeared outside. A couple more cooed and purred in the shadows, the way pigeons do. And though Erich had been inside the old church building hundreds of times before, he still paused to find his way.

"It's weird." He shook his head. "Everything's so different from what I remember. Scrambled and jumbled and wrecked."

"I don't like it." Katarina kept her arms crossed as she picked her way over a pile of bricks. Her shoes crackled on the broken colored window glass. "We're in big trouble if any of the Russian guards find us."

"Would you stop worrying? They don't ever come in here."

He hoped not, anyway. Once Erich had his bearings, he led the way over a collapsed section of wall and down a side hallway. Here and there they had to stop and crawl over piles of plaster rubble and cracked building stones and pieces of splintered beams.

"Careful." Erich helped his cousin over a pile near the end of a dark dead-end hallway and looked around. At the doorway to his father's little study, the charred door now hung by just a single hinge. Inside, a half-burned pile of papers and books had been swept into the corner, as if by a giant hand. Pigeons in the far corner stared at the intruders. Only one piece of furniture survived—his father's solid walnut desk—but it was mostly charred and had been crushed on one side by a fallen ceiling beam.

"Wow. It looks so different in here," Katarina whispered.

It seemed right to whisper in a place like this, like at a graveyard. Erich nodded then fell to his knees and began digging through the pile of papers and books.

"Your mother has never been back, has she?"

"Are you kidding?" He shook his head no. "Seeing all my father's stuff like this would kill her."

And what really was left? Nothing you could call a memory, exactly, not like what he was looking for. Only shredded records and damaged books. As he dug deeper, most of the paper fell apart at his touch. Deeper still, he found a few books that had survived with only a ripped spine or a blackened cover.

"Look at this." He held up a copy of an old theology book, mostly whole, and another that had been buried. That one had his father's name in the front, handwritten. He set it aside to take home. And the deeper he dug, the more books he found. Mostly in German, but a few in English, by authors like Dwight Moody and Brother Lawrence. And then—

"Luther," he whispered, and he held the book up with two fingers. Compared to most of the other stuff in the pile, it still looked okay. He blew the dust off and read the title on the cover.

Dr. Martin Luther's Sämtliche Schriften.

Collected Writings, the book his father had talked about just before he died.

But Erich wasn't sure what he would find inside: A note? An inscription? Maybe nothing but Luther's sermons. If nothing else, Erich would at least save this one, though it reeked of dust and mildew like everything else in the pile.

"Open it up!" Katarina leaned over his shoulder. Another book for her collection? She'd probably want to read it.

But not this one.

Erich whistled when he opened the book and discovered its hollowed-out insides. But hollowed out on purpose. Each page had been carefully cut, leaving a square hollow in the middle big enough to hide—

"It's a communion cup." Erich picked it out and held it up to the light. The silver cup looked tarnished and a bit smaller than usual—not much bigger than a cup that might hold a soft-boiled egg. "The kind pastors take with them to visit sick people."

"But why did he hide it in this book?" Katarina wondered. Erich had no idea, but he noticed something else inside the hollowed-out section.

"A little key!" The kind that might open a suitcase or a jewelry box.

Katarina pointed at it. "Just like in a mystery book."

"Huh?" Erich didn't follow.

"You know. The hero finds a mysterious key, and nobody knows what it fits until the end of the story, and then they find a treasure in a pirate chest. But you don't read those kinds of stories, do you?"

"Nope." Erich grunted, glancing around. "And I don't see any pirate chests in here."

"That's just in the stories, silly. There has to be a good reason your father hid this key in a place like this."

"And then he tried to tell my mother about it." This was beginning to sound more and more like one of Katarina's stories, after all. They'd have to do a little more searching to see if this key fit anything in the ruined study. But as Erich picked up the little key by its faded blue ribbon, they heard voices echoing down the hallway from the sanctuary.

"Shh!" Katarina tilted her head, as if that would help her hear better. She listened for a moment before whispering: "They're speaking Russian."

And they were getting closer.

"You sure?"

"We need to get out of here."

Erich didn't argue as he slipped his two new treasures into his pocket. He would come back for the books. But surely no one had seen them sneak inside the church, had they?

Wolfgang!

"This way." Katarina found her way past the half-crumpled desk and through a gaping hole in the wall of the study, back to the hallway. "Hurry!" Erich looked back to see a Russian soldier catch sight of them as they slipped around a corner. Erich stared at him for just an instant—long enough to see the man's black eyes and square jaw. He looked more like a shark than a man, and Erich felt more like a fish about to be eaten for lunch than a thirteen-year-old. Well, he had never seen a shark, but he'd seen pictures in school.

"You there!" shouted the Shark in thick-accented German. "Stop!"

Sorry, not this time. Erich and Katarina flew down the hallway and around two more corners, up a short flight of stairs, and right through a flock of pigeons.

"Whoa!" Erich held up his hands as dozens of wings batted him in the face. Katarina did the same, but was quicker to vault over a broken door to a back exit. A moment later Erich brushed the feathers out of his face as they burst outside and sprinted down Ackerstrasse, back toward Oma's apartment.

He didn't dare look back.

12

KAPITEL ZWÖLF

EMERGENCY CALL

FOUR WEEKS LATER . . .

"Oh!" Erich mumbled to himself as he opened their front door and stepped back to let Fred DeWitt inside.

Four times in four weeks.

But the airman pretended not to hear.

"Hey, bud!" DeWitt was all smiles, as usual, as he stepped into the tiny living room. And as usual he carried his bribe: another bag of food. "Your mom around?"

Well, that was a dumb question, and Erich let him know as much by looking around the room as if she might be. By way of a short hallway, the kitchen joined the living room, where his mother had set up a sheet curtain around her bedroll for privacy. She had pulled it back neatly before she left, though, and tied it off with a piece of colored yarn. Erich's blanket lay rolled up in the kitchen next to where he slept on the floor, and the little kitchen stood empty.

So no, she wasn't home. Obviously.

Neither of them said anything for a long, awkward moment. Of course, it wouldn't have been awkward if the guy would just leave them alone, if he would just leave Erich's mother alone.

"I guess that's a no." The sergeant didn't seem to let it get him down. "You expect her back very soon? She's off work, right?"

"She's out standing in some line to get more of that corn-meal stuff."

The stuff that made Erich want to throw up. The stuff that answered the question: what's worse than having nothing at all to eat?

"Oh. Well, listen, I feel bad about that." He set down his paper sack on the folding card table in the kitchen. "So I brought you some more stuff. Another can of peaches. You like those, right? And some canned tuna. You ever had tuna fish sandwiches?"

Erich stared at him blankly. He didn't mean to be rude, but he just couldn't pretend to be this man's friend, no matter how often Katarina told him he should try.

"Hmm," DeWitt said and then went on. "Anyway, you just mix it up with some mayo, see?" He paused. "Right; you don't have mayo. Well, you don't have to mix it up with anything. You can just serve it straight on a piece of bread."

Another pause as he thought that one through too.

"Right. No bread, either. Well ... you don't need to add anything at all. You can just eat it straight out of the can. How does that sound?"

Erich shrugged and the American smiled.

"There you go. It's all I could bring you right now, but I'll get some more on my ration card next week, soon as I can."

"Thanks." Erich nodded, still holding the open door, hoping the man would get the message.

Instead, DeWitt crossed his arms and leaned against the wall.

"Listen, I know we got off to a rough start, and—"

Erich didn't look at the man. He studied his shoes as DeWitt continued.

"—and I don't know exactly what happened here, but maybe we can start all over, huh? I introduce myself, you introduce yourself, like we never met, see?" He put out his hand. "Hi, I'm Fred DeWitt from Cleveland, Ohio. Pleased to meet you."

Erich didn't shake the outstretched hand of the man from Clevelandohio; he just bit his lip and, without thinking, looked up at the photo of his dad on the wall. It looked like the one in Oma's apartment, only in this one his father wore his pastor's robe, looking proud and excited and grinning from ear to ear. Erich's mother had told him it was taken the day his father was ordained as a pastor.

"Ohh, I get it." DeWitt nodded as he lowered his hand, but he didn't get it. The American didn't get anything. "You think

I'm trying to elbow my way in here and steal your mom away, is that it?"

Erich didn't answer. He looked down again and could almost see his own reflection in the guy's black military shoes. And he kept his arms crossed as DeWitt stumbled on.

"Listen, Erich, I don't have any ... That is to say, I'm not ... I'm just trying to—"

Trying to what? Erich waited while the American tried to untie his tongue. But it wasn't as much fun to watch as Erich might have expected. With a sigh and a "Skip it!" DeWitt finally gave up and headed for the door.

"Oh, by the way." He reached into his shirt pocket and pulled out a folded newspaper clipping. "My picture—I mean, *your* picture, you and your cousin catching that parachute candy that we got Fletcher to drop out of his plane? It got picked up by the *New York Times*, which, if you don't know, is a really big deal. Page three"—he tapped the clipping—"right next to the article about how the airlift brings this Cold War right back to the Russians."

"Oh."

"Look, I just want you to understand I wasn't trying to use you and your cousin for a big story. I'm not trying to get you mixed up in the politics of this whole thing. That's just the way it turned out, and I apologize for making you ... I don't know."

"What kind of politics?" Erich didn't quite follow.

"Oh. You know, the Russians against the Americans stuff. The Cold War. Well, look around you." He pointed out the window at a C-54 dropping from the sky on its final approach to Tempelhof. "That's the Cold War, right there. Us versus them. Like it or not, we're right in the middle of it."

That part, Erich understood. Maybe more than DeWitt knew. But the American wasn't finished.

"It's just that the pictures turned out better than anybody expected, and now my editor wants more. A follow-up story on the kids of the Berlin Airlift, right? People back in the States are eating it up."

Erich had to think about that one for a moment. The sergeant was always saying things in a funny way.

Eating it up?

DeWitt held out the clipping once more. "So, anyway, I thought you'd want your own copy. For your scrapbook, huh?"

"Thank you." This time Erich forced himself to be polite, but he couldn't think of anything else to say, and he didn't have a scrapbook. DeWitt rubbed his forehead for a moment and stepped into the hallway, which turned out to be perfect timing.

"Fred!" When Erich's mother saw DeWitt at the door, she nearly dropped her little parcel of rationed cornmeal. A smile lit up her face. "I was hoping you'd stop by. Will you stay for din—"

That's when she must have realized what she was holding.

"Oh, I mean ... if you don't mind cornmeal soup."

DeWitt glanced briefly at Erich and shook his head no.

"Thanks, uh, but no. Nothing against cornmeal, actually. Just wouldn't be right to eat your food. And I, uh, I have to get back to the base. But I left a couple of things on the kitchen table … thought you might, well—" He turned again to go, this time for real. Frau Kessler from across the hall poked her head out her door, checking to see what the American was doing. Erich's mother frowned, mostly at Erich.

"He's just leaving, Frau Kessler. And thank you, Fred." She started to wave with her free hand, then changed her mind and folded her fingers one by one before poking Erich in the ribs.

"Ow!" Erich yelped, but he knew what his mother wanted him to say. "I mean, thank you, Fred."

He wasn't sure DeWitt heard him, anyway. And he wasn't sure why he went to the living room window to watch the American step onto the sidewalk, look both ways, and hurry down the street.

But that's not what caught Erich's attention. He might not even have noticed if he hadn't seen the man move inside the old gray Mercedes.

Actually, it looked like two men. One in the driver's seat, the other putting on his hat and slipping out the passenger door to the far sidewalk. And when the passenger looked straight up at the window, Erich was quick enough to back away—but not before he got a pretty good look.

"Can't be." Erich caught a quick breath as he backed even farther into the living room and tried to think of what to do. Good thing his mother had already gone into the kitchen to see what DeWitt had brought them. Because he was willing to bet a whole can of peaches that he had seen the man before, back in the ruins of the *Versöhnungskirche*. Even from across the street, it was hard to miss the square jaw and dark eyes.

The only thing was, the man didn't have on a Russian uniform this time. In the American sector of Berlin, he'd better not. No telling what would happen to him if he were caught. Erich understood this part of the Cold War.

He just didn't understand why the Shark was following Fred DeWitt.

If it really *was* the Shark. Erich would have liked another look, just to be double-sure. But when he checked again, the car had gone. And thirty minutes later Erich had other things to worry about when he answered the urgent pounding at the door.

Erich cautiously opened the door. "Herr Kessler?"

The red-faced apartment manager pushed his way inside.

"Frau Becker!" Herr Kessler headed straight for the kitchen. "You'll want to hear about this urgent telephone message right away!"

"Urgent?" She looked up from the dishes in the sink. "Who sends us an urgent message?"

"That's just it!" Herr Kessler only got this worked up when the plumbing plugged up or the coal ran out. "He sounded Russian. But he didn't give his name."

"Well, that doesn't matter. Just tell me what he said." Erich's mother offered the man a sliver of canned peach on a plate. He licked his fingers after downing the treat, looking for more payment. And he got it. After all, the building manager and his wife, the spy, owned the only working telephone in the entire apartment building.

"He just said that he had visited your mother-in-law in her apartment and that she was in critical condition, that you should come quickly because the accident had been quite serious."

"Accident? Quite serious?" Frau Becker gasped and set the remaining canned peaches down on the table. "What did he mean by that? Did she fall? Does she need to go to the hospital?"

"I just take the telephone messages, Frau Becker." Herr Kessler kept his eyes on the can. "Although it does seem as if he said something else, perhaps. You don't happen to have any more of those American peaches, do you?"

"Mom!" Erich whispered, too late. His mother had already offered their building manager the last of the fruit.

"Help yourself, Herr Kessler," she told him. "It's the least we can do for your kindness."

"*Dankeschön.*" He smiled and inhaled the rest of the treat in one swift move before scratching his bald head. "Thanks so much. Now I remember."

"What do you remember?" Erich had to know too. "What did the doctor say?"

"Erich!" His mother scolded him while Herr Kessler wiped his mouth with the back of his hand.

"That was all, actually. He said nothing more before he hung up. I remember it clearly now."

Erich would have thrown the empty can at the man if his mother hadn't held him back.

"We're grateful to you, Herr Kessler." And two minutes later they were on their way to Oma's apartment once more, after leaving a message for Katarina's mother. At least the Mercedes hadn't returned to its parking spot across the street. Still, Erich checked up and down Oranienstrasse as they hurried to catch the S-Bahn, one of Berlin's streetcars.

"They'll be along," his mother told him. "They" meaning Katarina and her mother. "I think they're still waiting in a line somewhere."

Like everyone else in Berlin. But they would make it to Oma's soon. Erich checked over his shoulder once more, just to be sure no one else was following them.

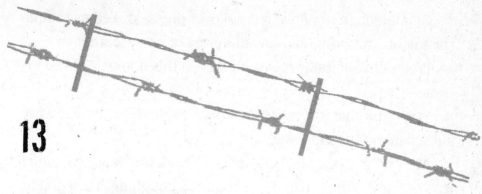

13

KAPITEL DREIZEHN

HELMUT WEISS, CHURCHMOUSE

"Brigitte?" Oma Poldi's face showed her surprise as she opened her door wide and motioned for them to step inside. "A pleasant surprise."

"Wait a minute." Erich's mother stopped short in the doorway. "What are you doing out of bed?"

"Bed? It's only eight o'clock, child. A summer night in August, and it's too warm to go to bed early. I may be old and sick, but—"

"No, but is the doctor still here? We came as soon as we could."

"Doctor? What doctor are you talking about?"

"The doctor that called our apartment house an hour ago," Erich explained. This was getting too strange. "The one who told Herr Kessler to tell us that we should come right away, that you might die."

Oma Poldi, in her flowered pullover dress, looked as though she might start coughing any minute. But near death?

"You didn't actually talk with this ... this doctor?" asked Oma.

Erich's mother shook her head no. "Only Herr Kessler, who passed along the message."

At this Oma Poldi leaned her head back and laughed, which was probably a mistake, as it set off her coughing. They had to wait several minutes while she caught her breath once again.

"I wonder if you gave him something for his trouble?" Oma finally asked, still wheezing.

"Of course."

"Nearly a half can of American peaches!" Erich put in.

"There, you see?" Oma had it figured out, this mystery. "Kessler is no fool, only a liar and a thief. He sees something he wants, and he finds a way for you to give it to him. So he makes up the story about me on my deathbed, which is not so far from the truth, after all, so you believe it. He makes up this pretend doctor, and the pretend urgent telephone call. You are in his debt. 'Oh, *dankeschön*; thank you so much, Herr Kessler. You will have some peaches, *bitte*?' Humph! Not such a mystery."

"That makes sense," replied Erich's mother, "except Herr Kessler didn't know about the peaches before he pounded on our door."

"If not peaches, then something else," replied Oma.

"But what about when we found out the truth?" Erich wondered. "Did he think we would just come home and say, 'Oh, well, that was a funny joke'? What would he do then?"

"Maybe he didn't think it through that far." Oma shrugged. "Men can be like that, you know."

Maybe. Erich still had a hard time believing old Herr Kessler was that good an actor, though. And he worried about who had really called them, and why. He couldn't shake the image of the Shark outside their apartment. But as far as the ladies were concerned?

"Well, never mind," said Oma. Then she offered to make tea for them, and they shared the few crackers Erich's mother had brought along.

"I'm going outside for a few minutes," Erich told them. He checked his pocket to make sure he still had the key. "To see if Katarina is coming."

Or maybe their friend Wolfgang would be waiting for him.

It didn't matter either way. Waiting for Katarina and her family gave him time to search his father's study again. This time without the Russians on his tail. He hurried outside, munching his half-cracker, keeping one eye over his shoulder.

Was that man a half-block behind following him? He couldn't tell. But when he stopped at an *apotheke,* a pharmacy, the shadow also stopped. And when he sped up, the shadow also sped up. He passed two Soviet guards, laughing and smoking on the corner of Ackerstrasse. They stood at attention as the shadow passed by them.

Not a good sign. And Erich could not forget where he was: in the Soviet sector.

Why did I come out here alone? he asked himself.

He sprinted around the corner in front of the church, ducked into an alley, and counted to *neunundneunzig,* ninety-nine. A mother walked by pushing a stroller. A couple of old people, going slow. A group of four young women, probably off work for the day. But no shadow.

So okay. He darted across the alley and approached the ruined church from the back, where he and Katarina had made their escape the other day. No one seemed to notice on a Thursday evening; everyone probably just wanted to be home. He pushed past a temporary fence and slipped inside.

And if it had seemed dark before, this time ... he held his hand out in front of him and felt the way with the toe of his shoe. At least he'd come prepared, with a candle stub and a single match. He would save them, though, until he approached his father's study once more. There! The candle flickered and cast a pale puddle of light, a meter to every side.

Once more he stood in his father's study, the same way he had when he'd been five or six, only it had seemed so much bigger then. Now it hardly seemed the same place. Then, his father would sit at his desk, writing sermons. His bookshelves covered the walls. Now, nothing looked right, and he could find nothing that would fit the key. Not even close. What did he expect? A magic door? After several minutes of fruitless searching he sighed and leaned against the wall.

"Why did I come here?" Hot wax dribbled onto his finger, and when he jerked back, the candle blinked out—just as a hand came down on his shoulder.

"I have no idea, preacher's boy. Why *did* you come here?"

Erich might have died right there if the man hadn't held on to his shoulder. And honestly, he tried to scream, but nothing came out of his mouth except a chattering "yaa-yaa-yaa!" Too bad Katarina wasn't here this time; she could have let loose with a real screech.

"Relax." The man spoke softly, as he might to a scared animal. He stepped back and lit a small candle lantern of his own. "You're not in trouble, not with me. Now, the Russians who were following you the other day, that could be another thing."

"You, you know who I am?" Erich croaked as he tried to get a closer look at the man's wrinkled face. But he had seen hundreds of men like him in Berlin. Scarecrows, really, with sad, hollow sockets for eyes and sunken cheeks that made them look like concentration camp survivors. The skin around his arms hung loosely, as if he had once filled out his frame much better.

"You don't remember, of course." A shadow passed across the man's expression as he looked up and around. "I used to clean this building, keep the furnace lit, dust the altar. That kind of thing."

Once he got used to the man's toothless lisp, Erich could follow the words plainly. And yes, he *did* remember, though faintly. A large round man who laughed, an old man even back then. The maintenance man, Herr—

"Helmut Weiss." He nodded when he said it, the way a doorman or a train conductor might. "Glad to serve you."

Glad to serve me? As if he had stumbled upon some long-lost family butler. But yes.

"My mother—" A ghost of a thought tickled the edge of Erich's memory. "My mother used to pack little *pfeffernusse* cookies for my father's lunch. Well, they weren't really *pfeffernusse*, since we didn't have any sugar or eggs. But she tried. I would bring them at lunchtime, and we would leave some for you on a plate."

The man chuckled and closed his eyes. "You *do* remember."

"But what are you doing here? And how did I not hear you come up behind me?"

In other words, what kind of ghost had he met in this spooky old church?

"I live here, young Master Becker." He carefully scooted a twisted book aside with his foot. "Actually, not in this room, but in another, that is, in the basement. I've learned to get around."

Erich shivered to think of someone actually living here, someone watching him and Katarina as they walked through the building, someone slipping through the shadows.

"Isn't it cold and damp?"

"I don't mind so much, living as a churchmouse. No one bothers me. And the pigeon eggs, well, they're small, but tasty. Perhaps you'd like to try some?"

"Nein, danke." Erich shuddered and tried not to look at the man's haunted face. "No, thanks. I was just looking for—"

But he couldn't finish the sentence, and his hand went to the key once more. Maybe Herr Weiss could help him. Maybe not. Erich wasn't sure if he could take the chance. Better to ask questions than tell secrets. The old man held up his lantern and looked at Erich more closely.

"You look just like your father, you know." That seemed an odd thing to say in a place like this, in the ruins of his father's life and work. "Your father was a good man."

"He was, until the Americans did all this." Erich couldn't help kicking at a stray piece of plaster. "Until they killed him with their bombs."

Herr Weiss said nothing for a long moment, only breathed in through his mouth, making a raspy wheezing sound.

"This is what they told you? That your father was killed in a bombing raid?"

Erich felt himself tense up, as if he'd put up his fists. Who was this man, really? What was he saying?

"Isn't that what happened?"

Herr Weiss turned deadly serious, and the look on his face made Erich shiver.

"Listen to me, young man. Your father was not killed by an American bomb, and his death was no accident."

"What do you know about that?"

Did Erich really want to know? This was getting ridiculous, this strange meeting in a ruined church. Was this man crazy? But once more Herr Weiss turned quiet, and when he spoke again, Erich had to lean closer to hear him.

"I can't tell you the whole story, but this much I know: your father was involved with something … something against the Nazis. A plot of some kind. Something very dangerous. They came to ask him questions many times. And the last day you saw him?"

By that time Erich was nearly face-to-face with the man, hanging on every word.

"He was not killed here in the bombs. *They* took him away."

Erich didn't need to ask who *they* were. The Gestapo—Hitler's secret police. So it wasn't the Americans, as he had believed for so long?

Erich finally broke away, shaking his head. "I don't believe you." He stumbled backward and sat down hard on a pile of books. "You're just making up stories."

Herr Helmut Weiss looked at him with his sad, sunken eyes. He held out his hand to help Erich to his feet.

"I wish I were, Master Becker. I wish I were."

So did Erich. Maybe it was the sad shock of what Helmut Weiss had told him. Or the look in his eyes. Either way, Erich could not stop the tears, as if they had been stored up for all these years. Now he knew, and he wished he didn't. It had been easier just being mad at the Americans.

He turned away and buried his face. And as his shoulders shook with sobs he felt the horrible weight of this new truth. Love your enemies? Easy for Katarina to say. But he'd been so good at hating these people, maybe too good. Now, if he was honest, he couldn't think of a reason to keep it up, anymore.

I miss you, Papa.

After a couple of minutes, he gulped for air and tried to dry his eyes on the dusty sleeve of his shirt. When he felt ready to stand, he reached for Herr Weiss's outstretched hand—just as the man stiffened and turned his head.

"What's wrong?" Erich didn't hear anything. But like a bat in a cave, Herr Weiss seemed to know.

"Someone's come in the front doors." His whisper blew out the candle. "You will leave the back way again, as you did the other day. Quickly!"

There would be no argument with Herr Weiss, who disappeared the same way he had appeared—without a sound. Erich had no idea how someone could be so quiet. He felt his way out of the room, praying that whoever had entered the church would make more noise than he did. Once again Erich left the Reconciliation Church with more questions than answers.

14

KAPITEL VIERZEHN

BORDER STANDOFF

"Too bad you couldn't have asked that man more questions." Katarina kept her voice down that late-summer night as they walked ahead of their mothers by a few steps. Another half-block and they'd be back in the American sector, almost home.

"Well, you should have been there, then. I didn't have a chance." Erich dragged his feet a little, which wasn't so odd, considering everything that had already happened that night. And though it would have been nicer if they'd had the money to ride a tram this time, it really hadn't taken long for them to walk the mile and a half from Oma's apartment. Just long enough to tell Katarina everything that had happened in the church—from the stranger in the shadows who had followed him, to the odd church janitor who had told him about his father.

Her eyes grew wider with each detail as they neared his apartment building on Oranienstrasse. They could almost see it, on the other side of the line between the American and Soviet sectors, which sort of wandered through this neighborhood. Except for the signs, you couldn't always tell just by looking where one sector stopped and the other began.

But Katarina held back.

"What's wrong?" asked her mother, bumping into them from behind. Katarina pointed up ahead.

"Someone," she whispered, and Erich followed her gaze to see someone sitting in the shadows of the apartment building's front steps.

"Is that Fred?" Frau Becker's step lightened. "I hope he hasn't been waiting for us all this time."

Well, he might have. But whoever had been there disappeared just as a car parked on the Soviet sector side came to life and raced at them, its lights on full bright. They jumped out of the way, but the old gray Mercedes bumped onto the sidewalk. Erich's mother held her hands in front of her face as the car shrieked to a stop. A man stepped out to meet them.

"Pardon the interruption, Frau Becker." The uniformed man stepped in front of them to block their way. Erich gasped when he saw the square-jawed outline and the black shark eyes, the twin row of buttons on his uniform jacket and the peaked military hat. No telling what rank this man was, though clearly he was some kind of officer. "We've been wanting to speak with you and your son for quite some time."

Well, then you certainly made the grand entrance, didn't you? Erich didn't dare speak the words.

But his mother didn't shrink back. "Who are you? And how do you know my name?" She kept a hand on her purse and the other on Erich's arm. Katarina and her mother held back in the shadows. And the dim glow from a nearby streetlight caught the man's toothy grin as he bowed his head slightly.

"Captain Viktor Yevchenko, at your service. And if you've forgotten where you are, I'd be happy to remind you." He still blocked the way, only ten feet away from the American sector. Ten feet away from freedom.

"We know where we are," Erich answered him.

"Then perhaps you also know that in this part of the city *we* will ask the questions. And for the time being, you will consider yourselves our guests."

"A guest would get an invitation, right?" Erich blurted out. And even though his mother shushed him, he had to know. "You're the one who called today. The phony doctor. Isn't that true?"

A wild guess? The shark eyes twinkled for a moment, and Captain Yevchenko grinned again as he looked at Frau Becker.

"Your son is very bright. We'll have much to discuss, the three of us. You other two—" He snapped his fingers at Katarina and her mother, dismissing them as he would a servant. "You will go home now, please."

"We're not leaving our family." Katarina's mom planted her feet.

Which was awfully nice of her to say, just maybe not the best timing. Erich glanced over at his cousin, and for a moment he thought they shared the same idea. They could outrun him. But what about their mothers? She shook her head, and he knew she was right.

As if reading his mind, a uniformed Russian bodyguard stepped from the car. Even in the dark, Erich could see this was the kind of guy who filled out the uniform pretty well. His neck looked as wide as his head. And he made sure they could see the blunt gray rifle slung over his shoulder like a guitar, his finger on the trigger. So much for the idea of running away.

"Oh, yes, you will leave." This time Captain Yevchenko wagged a finger at Katarina and her mother. "Immediately, please. Your friends will be back home in no time at all."

"I demand to know what this is all about!" Erich's mother dared to raise her voice, though the Russian hardly blinked, only pointed his square jaw at her.

"You're quite a talented actress, Frau Becker. But let's stop playing the innocent bystander, shall we?"

When she didn't answer, he went on.

"Or perhaps your son should tell you what he's been doing searching through forbidden buildings and restricted areas. Did you know about that? Surely you already know about his association with the American agent, since you seem to have frequent contact with the spy yourself."

"The spy?" she whispered.

"Humor me just a little, Frau Becker. We're talking about the American who drops propaganda by parachute into the Soviet sector. The one with the camera who is responsible for so much anti-Socialist propaganda. He's using you for his own purposes, woman. Or maybe you don't see past the cigarettes and the nylon stockings he brings you."

The words hit Erich like a slap in the face. DeWitt. This was all about Fred DeWitt. Did the Soviets really believe the American was a spy, or were they just sore at him for making such a big deal about the gum drop, making them look bad?

"Now, please," he went on. "It's late, and I have been waiting far too long." This time he grabbed Erich's arm and pointed to where the guard stood by an open car door. "You will come with us now."

"Let go!" Gun or no gun, Erich wasn't going to just get into the car without a fight. He dug in his heels and squirmed, whipping his arms around and trying his best to land a good punch. Captain Yevchenko was more than ready for him, though. And his arms were longer than they had looked, plenty long enough to hold Erich off. He simply twisted the collar of Erich's shirt until Erich fell to his knees and gasped for breath.

"You're making this rather difficult for everyone, Erich." Captain Yevchenko wasn't even sweating. "Now straighten up and act like a man. You can help us."

"Noooo!" Naturally his mother came to the rescue, but by that time the bodyguard had stepped up with his gun and jabbed it hard into Erich's side. "Oh!" Erich doubled over with pain as tears came to his eyes. And Frau Becker would probably have grabbed the rifle if the bodyguard hadn't hit her across the cheek with the back of his gloved hand, sending her tumbling to the ground.

"Nobody hits my mom!" Erich tried to face the man but felt his legs buckle beneath him. He didn't think Jesus had this kind of thing in mind when he said to turn the other cheek. Or did he?

"That's enough." This time the command came from an American. And Erich had to say that for the first time ever, Fred DeWitt's voice sounded wonderful. Beautiful, even. Erich curled up and hugged his side, trying not to sob or throw up, while his mother held her arm around him.

"Sergeant DeWitt!" Captain Yevchenko sounded glad to see him. "I was wondering how long it would take for you to join us. This is good. I'm sure we will have a fruitful discussion on matters of mutual interest. If you come a little closer, you might find that we can help each other."

"Tell your thug to back away from these people." DeWitt didn't sound like he was in the mood for a fruitful discussion.

Captain Yevchenko sighed. "Ah, but I think you're forgetting which side of the border you're on. Remember that over there, you can do nothing. You can't set one polished boot over here. In fact, I can't even seem to hear you, and that's quite a shame, isn't it?"

"Then maybe you can hear this."

Everyone froze when they heard the plain *click* of a gun, ready to fire, a sound that seemed to echo through the now-deserted street. Erich looked up slowly to see that DeWitt still stood planted in the American sector. But the serious military handgun he pointed at Captain Yevchenko could surely hit its target from ten feet.

"Now, let's do this slowly," came DeWitt's steady voice again. "I want your friend to set his rifle down on the street, and both of you to get back into your car."

"You have no right! We're simply attending to state security matters." Yevchenko's expression had turned to stone.

"It's a little tough to find the exact border in some places, don't you think?" DeWitt's aim remained steady. "I might cross over by mistake."

"You're not serious. Now let's just—"

"You don't want to find out how serious I am."

DeWitt's voice told anybody listening that he wasn't kidding. And after a couple of strained words from Captain Yevchenko, the Russian weapon clattered to the pavement. Erich didn't want to touch the rifle, but now that he'd caught his breath he didn't mind kicking it away, out of reach. It stuck barrel-first into a heavy steel grate of a gutter storm drain, which gave him an idea. Ignoring the burning pain in his side, he got up and grabbed the wooden stock, yanking up with all his strength. As he'd hoped, the steel grate held the business end of the rifle in place, and he had just enough leverage to bend the end of the barrel slightly. He pulled it free and tossed it back toward the car, twisted and useless.

"I always thought it would be fun to be able to shoot around corners," Erich told them. "Now you can try it."

DeWitt raised his eyebrows but held his own gun steady.

"The gun is of no consequence." A black fire still glowed in Captain Yevchenko's eyes, and he lowered his voice so that only the two of them could hear. "But I do fear for your safety, young man. And that of your American friend."

With that, Captain Yevchenko picked up the useless rifle and returned to the car with his bodyguard. And though each breath felt like the stab of a fire poker in his ribs, Erich knew he had to help his mother to safety. Katarina and her mother scurried away, as well.

"Don't tell me you read a book like this once." Erich took his cousin by the arm as they hurried to the safety of the Beckers' apartment. DeWitt would follow them, while the Russians' car left with a squeal of tires and cloud of smoke.

"No." Katarina wasn't saying much, just shaking her head. She looked almost as pale as his mother. "I haven't ever read anything like this."

"Are you all right, Mama?" He looked to his mother, who had collapsed in tears on the stairway halfway up to the second floor. DeWitt bounded up to help them back to their apartment. Erich pretended his side didn't hurt as he brought a damp washrag for his mother. Her cheekbone was already turning purple where Captain Yevchenko's thug had hit her.

"Don't let those jerks scare you." DeWitt had to be trying awfully hard to sound so cool and collected. "Although you probably shouldn't go visit the Soviet side again anytime soon."

Erich knew he'd better tell them where he'd seen the Russian pair once before, here on their own street, in the middle of the day. But as he watched DeWitt, he couldn't bring himself to say it. Another question burned his tongue.

Since when had DeWitt the newspaperman started carrying a gun?

15

KAPITEL FÜNFZEHN

THE ANNOUNCEMENT

THREE MONTHS LATER . . .

One good thing about their little apartment: from their kitchen window (and even a little bit from the living room), Erich had no trouble following the parade of C-54's coming in for landings at Tempelhof, which he thought was a lot more interesting than doing math homework. Especially when they'd let go with a load of candy parachutes once every couple of days for three whole months: September, October, and November. Even his mother liked to watch and remind them how much she loved chocolate, and would *someone* run out there and get her some?

So it didn't matter how noisy the planes turned out to be. On the other hand, a lot of other noises came through their thin walls just as easily. Herr Meyer belching below them. Frau

Braun's yappy dog next door, who barked at shadows. (There had been a lot of shadows in November.) And now his mother in the other room, arguing with Fred DeWitt after a quiet Friday dinner.

Excuse me, *bitte*? Did they think Erich couldn't hear them from the kitchen?

"I'm just saying perhaps we should work things out better before we make such a decision." Frau Becker sounded more tired than angry. Fred DeWitt just sounded confused.

"I don't understand. Yesterday we agreed, but now today?"

"Fred, you understand what I'm saying. It just seems like everyone is against us."

"Name one person."

"Your grandparents in Ohio. That's two. Also my mother-in-law, when I checked on her last week. She smiles and says it's all fine, but I can tell."

"You went over there again?"

"I had no choice, Fred. No one followed me. Maybe they've forgotten."

"I still don't like it."

"Even so, you ask who is against us. What about your commanding officer? And I didn't even mention Heinz."

"Oh, Heinz; come on. Since when do you have to get an okay from your older brother to get married? He's Communist, for crying out loud."

Erich caught his breath at the words. One, because his mother never talked about Uncle Heinz. All Erich knew was that his mother's brother had worked in Moscow for a few years, and they hadn't heard from him, well, until now. Definitely the black sheep of the family.

And of course the other thing that stopped his heart was the "M" word. Make that the "H" word in German. *Heirat.* Marriage. Had Erich really heard them right?

Erich's mother didn't answer right away. But when she did she sounded far away and weepy.

"I'm sorry, Fred. Everything's happened too fast. I know we need to trust God, and we can't worry so much about what other people are saying. But still. When your commanding officer says that he'll do everything in his power to prevent you from marrying a German woman, doesn't that concern you?"

"Bigots don't concern me. All that concerns me is serving God and marrying you."

"You'd better be careful how you talk about your commanding officer, Sergeant DeWitt." But she giggled when she said it. By this time Erich was pretty sure they'd forgotten he was in the apartment. He wasn't sure if he should clear his throat so they'd hear him, move closer to the wall so he could catch every word, or plug his ears and start humming to himself. Option A, B, or C.

He chose option A, except he knocked into one of the kitchen chairs on his way to the short hallway between the two rooms.

"Oh, Erich!" His mother looked up at him with wide eyes when he picked himself up and stepped into the living room. "I thought you were outside."

"Well, I was this afternoon," he reminded her, "but then I came in for dinner. Remember?"

Remember, Fred DeWitt came over for dinner, the same way he had been doing for the past several months? Remember the can of American pork and beans he'd brought with him? Her face flushed for a moment as Erich headed for the door.

"Maybe I'll go see what Katarina is doing," he mumbled.

"No, wait, Erich." DeWitt had been pacing by the threadbare sofa. "Your mother and I have something we need to tell you."

Erich didn't like the way that sounded, not at all. *Your mother and I.* He gritted his teeth and braced himself against the wall, the way an old guy might if he were expecting a heart attack. This would be worse.

"I already heard." Erich looked at the floor. Why did it come as such a shock? Maybe Fred DeWitt wasn't such a bad guy, after all. For an American, that is. Ever since the standoff with the Russians, Erich had learned to see some of the man's better side. DeWitt seemed to care about them. He'd been to church with them, said he loved Jesus, and Erich didn't have any real reason to doubt the man's word, other than the fact that he was an American. At least DeWitt always acted like a gentleman around Erich's mother, which was more than he could say for some of the other soldiers he'd met.

And his mother seemed to like him. A lot. This is what people did who really liked each other. Erich couldn't get himself to use the word *love,* though, not for anything. Just couldn't, because he still guarded a part of his heart somewhere, still kept the door closed and locked. But this was his mother's heart they were talking about. His didn't matter.

"You didn't hear the whole story, though, Erich."

"What's to know?" He pinched his lips together so he could spit out the words a little easier. "You want to get married. You should get ... married."

His mom glanced at DeWitt before turning back to him with a "please listen" in her eyes. All right, then. For her.

"I'm resigning the service," DeWitt told Erich. "I'm not going to re-enlist."

"Oh." That wasn't quite what Erich had expected to hear, but all right. "So what are you going to do?"

"Not just *him,* Erich." Erich's mother tilted her head to help get her point across. "Us. It's what *we're* going to do from now on. And we want you to be a part of that decision."

"Wha-what kind of decision?" Erich felt his heart race as he began to understand. As if he were in a tunnel and he saw the train coming straight at him. Because if Fred DeWitt wasn't going to be in the Air Force anymore, he would go home to Clevelandohio. And not just *him*—

"We can get married here in the *missionskirche,*" his mother went on. The Lutheran Mission Church. Of course not the Reconciliation Church, where his parents had been married, where Erich hadn't been since last summer.

"And then what?" He turned away so they wouldn't see his tears, which welled up out of nowhere. "Are you going to go to the United States? Is that what you're saying? Leave Berlin?"

"Would that really be so bad, Erich?" his mother's voice pleaded now. "You know this hasn't been an easy time, or an easy place to live. Not during the war and not since."

"But things have been getting better, haven't they? And Oma always says this is home, no matter what."

Erich crossed his arms, remembering how stubborn his grandmother could be. Stubborn about living. And stubborn about dying.

Well, he could be just as stubborn.

"Did you hear what I'm trying to tell you?" His mother's voice faded back to the present. "I ... that is, we want you to be as excited about this decision as we are."

Erich swallowed hard and nodded. Next they would tell him how much he would like Clevelandohio. Well, maybe so and maybe not. But in his heart he knew this was not a battle he would win, wasn't even sure it was a battle he wanted to fight anymore. A few months ago, maybe ... probably. Yes. But not now. And when he looked back at his mother's hopeful, tear-brimmed eyes, he knew he would not hurt her by digging in his heels.

"You understand what your mother is saying, don't you, Erich?" DeWitt looked him straight in the eyes, expecting an answer that Erich didn't have words for yet.

"I still have a lot of things to figure out."

What else could he say? His mother started to shake her head, warning DeWitt not to push anymore.

"I understand." The man rested his hand on Erich's shoulder. Big mistake. Erich shook free and headed for the door before he said something dumb, something he would be sorry for later.

"You don't understand anything." *No, no, no.* He bit his tongue. He'd only meant to think it, not say the words out loud. But his tongue seemed to have its own mind.

"Wait a minute, Erich. We're not done here."

"Fred, no." This time Erich's mother took DeWitt's arm, but the military man wasn't through.

"I don't know about you," Erich snapped, and wished it hadn't come out sharp enough to cut, "but *I'm* done."

Erich pulled at the door. *Out, out.* Anywhere but here. Before his mother started crying. Didn't DeWitt see? But DeWitt didn't see; he just parked his toe to stop the door.

"Why do you always think I'm stupid, Erich? You really think I haven't lived at all? That I don't know what you're thinking?"

"I don't think you're stupid." Erich tugged at the doorknob. "I just don't think you understand me. You speak German, but—"

"Yeah, well, you're not the only guy on the planet who ever lost his dad. Did you know mine left when I was twelve? So I think I know just a little bit of what you've been going through. If you'd just stop running away—"

Erich stared at the door as DeWitt's words echoed through the room.

"I didn't know that," he finally breathed and let the doorknob go. He felt low enough to crawl under the closed door. Instead, he wandered over to the window.

"You weren't supposed to. But I'll tell you, kid ... maybe we have more in common than you think."

"Maybe." And this time he didn't tense up just because DeWitt rested a hand on his shoulder. He tensed because of what he saw on the street below, through the window.

"Erich," his mother told him, "I know it's a big adjustment. We can talk about it some more later."

But Erich hardly heard her as he backed away from the window. After all these months, why now?

"The Russians," he whispered. "They're back."

"Are you sure?" DeWitt moved to the side of the window and peered out from behind the curtain. "I don't see anything now."

Erich peeked again, and the car had disappeared. Was he seeing things?

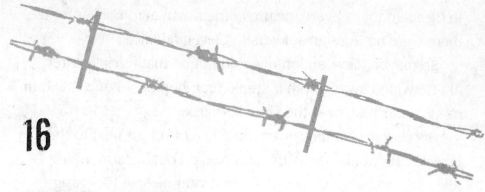

16

KAPITEL SECHZEHN

LAST GOOD-BYE

This time Erich didn't care if the Russians followed him or not,
or whether he had really seen them or not. What did he have to
tell them, anyway? They were wasting their time, following the
wrong person. He ran with his head down, faster and faster
until his lungs could not keep up with his legs, and he finally
had to stop and breathe. By that time a drizzle had soaked
through his shirt, but he didn't care about that, either. Didn't
care about the tears that ran down his cheeks and mixed with
the rain.

He had been right about one thing.

He did still have a lot of things to figure out, a lot of things
to think through. Would going with his mother and DeWitt to
Clevelandohio really be so bad? He sighed. Maybe not. DeWitt
said that in Clevelandohio people didn't go to bed hungry. In
Clevelandohio, the buildings weren't all bombed out and empty.

In Clevelandohio, everyone drove their own automobiles, and there were no Russian soldiers in Clevelandohio.

So maybe Clevelandohio would not be that terrible, after all. He wiped away another stupid tear, hoping no one saw him on Ackerstrasse, near the *Versöhnungskirche*.

His church. But movement on a pile of rubble next to the church caught his eye as the sun peeked out once more. An alley cat, probably. Or not. A second later he saw Wolfgang tumble down the pile without a word and run in the opposite direction, down the *strasse*, and around the corner.

Well. Not that he'd wanted to chat with Wolfgang anyway. But what had sent him running? He looked up and down the *strasse* once more before he slipped through the gap in the fence and found his way back into the *kirche*.

For the last time?

Quietly he picked his way down the hall, wondering what it took to get Weiss the Churchmouse's attention. If he tiptoed, surely the man would not hear him.

But what was he doing here? Hoping for wisdom from his father? Saying good-bye? He stood in the entry to his father's study, and once more he could not help feeling very small and young and stupid. The key in his pocket didn't fit some special treasure. What was he thinking? It just reminded him of what he could not have. He pulled out the key, squeezed it in his fist. And without thinking about it, he flung it across the room.

Good-bye. And I'm sorry for the way it turned out. Sorry I didn't keep my promise to take care of Mom as well as I should have. *Sorry I failed.* He couldn't say the words out loud, but he meant them all the same, and he turned to go. Even though—

No. Even if it didn't fit anything, the key had belonged to his father, had been held by his father. He would keep it. He'd take it to America and keep it with him always. Erich turned back and stepped over the rubble to the wall where the key had landed with a *plink.* Had it bounced under the collapsed desk? He got down on his knees to look for it. A little bit of gray light filtered in through the hole in the ceiling here, just enough to let him see—

—a small keyhole on the underside of the desk! It was where his father would have once parked his knees. How had he not seen it before? Only now that he had found the keyhole, what about the key?

"Oh, brother." He searched a few more minutes with no luck. *Maybe the key didn't land near the desk,* he thought. *Maybe it went down inside the hollow plaster wall and dropped down to who-knows-where.* He backed out from under the desk, bumping his head with a crack as he did.

"Owww!" He squinted in pain, but the hollow cracking sound wasn't so much his head as the desk itself. Maybe—

He lay down under the desk again. Using the heel of his hand, he slammed as hard as he could into the wood panel with the little keyhole, his father's hiding place. Let the Churchmouse hear him; he didn't care.

Crack! He tried again and again, and each time the wood gave way just a little more. Two more times, three, and the seam began to open. Four times, five, and his hand ached from the hammering, until the small door finally gave way. A little cloth bag fell onto his chest.

He could not move, his heart hammered so. But after checking to make sure the rest of the little compartment was empty, he finally crawled out from beneath the desk and emptied the little bag onto the floor. He felt like a pirate there in the ruined building, pouring out a small river of silver *reichsmark* coins in the last light of the day.

Thirty-three, thirty-four, thirty-five … He counted again, just to be sure he wasn't imagining it. Katarina would surely tell him she had read a story like this once, and it seemed far too unreal. Real people didn't find thirty-five *reichsmarks* in a compartment of a splintered desk, did they? He wasn't sure what such a treasure was worth today, but it didn't matter. Surely his father had meant for it to help him and his mother in an emergency, even in a small way.

Now it all made sense! Look in Luther for the key, and the key opened the little coin stash under the desk. Except his father didn't have a chance to tell them the whole story before he'd been killed by the Nazis. Not the Americans. Not the air raid. Not the bombs.

Well, no matter how much it was worth, his mother could use the money. Maybe it would buy them a new suit of clothes when they made it to Clevelandohio. Or a new car? He focused on scooping the coins back into the little bag, until he noticed that a cloud had slipped in front of the sun, darkening the room.

Actually, not a cloud. Erich looked up to see the Russian officer with the shark black eyes, hands on his hips, bigger than life. There would be no slipping by this man.

Captain Viktor Yevchenko, at your service.

"Erich Becker." The man dusted off his hands as if he had been infected by stepping inside the ruined house of worship. "I'm very pleased to have finally caught up with you ... after all these months."

Pleased was not a word Erich would have used within spitting distance. He palmed the coin bag and slipped it into his pocket as he stood. In time?

"Why have you been following me?" asked Erich.

Captain Yevchenko sighed and rolled his eyes.

"Perhaps you've already forgotten our meeting on the street a few months back? Though I regret the negative impression I must have made on you and your family."

"You hurt my mother."

"An unfortunate misunderstanding." Captain Yevchenko held up a hand. "Pasternov was reprimanded for being so rough with you, and I apologize. I hope it will not be necessary again."

"Right." Erich squeezed his lips together in a silent prayer and wondered what he was supposed to say to that. How about "I need to go."

But Captain Yevchenko didn't move out of the way, only pretended they were having a pleasant conversation. What *did* he want?

"Now you're wondering why I'm here, perhaps." From this angle he looked almost sorry to be there. "I think you will understand very soon. Now turn around."

Erich blinked. What?

"I said turn around! Please. I don't want you to be hurt."

Erich had no idea what would happen next. He only knew that he couldn't just stand there and let it happen. Why couldn't Katarina have been here this time? He lunged for the door, but the Russian must have been expecting it. As Erich hollered and kicked, Captain Yevchenko spun him around, pinned his arms against his back, and forced him to his knees, leaving Erich gasping for breath.

"I am so sorry," the man apologized once more as he taped Erich's wrists together with electrical tape. Then he wound the tape around Erich's head and over his mouth. "This will only be for a short while. Is that too tight?"

Erich leaned up against the wall, still stunned by the ferocious wrestling moves that left him helpless and silent on the floor. And why? He glanced up at the man for a clue.

"Please let me assure you one more time." Captain Yevchenko lowered himself to Erich's level. "I regret having to put you through this. It's just that we need your help right now."

Erich didn't bother trying to argue the point, not with his mouth taped shut. He was still trying to breathe.

"In fact, I have two girls, not much younger than you, back home in Moscow. Two lovely girls with no mother; now they stay with my sister."

For a moment he sounded like a real person, and for a moment his black eyes softened as he spoke of people he cared about. So the Shark had a soul, though he hid it behind the anger of his next question. "And do you know who killed their mother?"

Erich could guess. This had something to do with what the German army did. Captain Yevchenko took a deep breath and sighed.

"But I leave the past behind. Now we build for the future, and we have much to look forward to. It is now only the Americans who stand in our way." He raised his voice, as if giving a speech. "They stand in the way of a unified Germany. And they stand in the way of a unified Socialist world."

So now it was the Americans against the Communists. This Cold War that DeWitt always talked about. But Captain Yevchenko still had his point to make, and he lowered his face to look straight at Erich. Erich could close his eyes, but it would do no good.

"Your only mistake, Erich Becker, is making friends with the wrong man, with the wrong side. The side that can never win. Your American spy friend, Sergeant DeWitt? You might know who he really is, or you might not. That is not the point, because now we are left with only one way to deal with him. I have been waiting for this chance for many weeks."

He straightened up once more, washing his hands in the air.

"And I give you my word, you will be free to go after we deal with him."

What did this mean, this dealing *with DeWitt?* Erich shivered at the thought and wondered what he had to do with it, tied up like this. He tried to wiggle his wrists, now tingly and numb, when a pair of feet appeared at the door.

"Comrade Wolfgang." Captain Yevchenko turned to meet the boy, and Erich could only gasp when he remembered how Wolfgang had seen him coming down the street.

Comrade?

Wolfgang the Lookout stood at the door with no expression on his face, as if he saw people tied up like this every day. Meanwhile, Captain Yevchenko pulled a small pad and pencil from his uniform pocket and wrote something, thinking for a moment, then looking to Erich.

"*Allein* is the right word in German, is it not? By himself with no others? Yes, of course. *Allein,* alone. The sergeant will come *alone,* immediately, to guarantee the safety of the boy." He looked up from his note. "This is something he will understand, will he not? Let us hope so."

Erich could hear no more of this, but when he tried to get to his feet, Captain Yevchenko pushed him back to the floor. And so Erich could do nothing but lie with his face in the shreds of his father's library. He looked up in time to see Captain Yevchenko tear off his note and hand it to Wolfgang the Robot, Wolfgang the Zombie, who said not a word.

"Hurry, now." Captain Yevchenko patted his comrade on the shoulder. "We don't want Erich to be uncomfortable on the floor."

Erich would have screamed if he thought it would do any good. Instead, he worked his wrists, trying to loosen the tape. And just an inch from his face, behind a pile of shredded books, he spotted the little key.

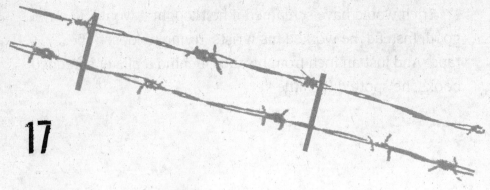

17

KAPITEL SIEBZEHN

COME ALONE

At least Captain Yevchenko hadn't noticed his father's collection of coins. That should make Erich feel a lot better, lying facedown in the ruins of the *Versöhnungskirche*.

Oh, and knowing where the key was made Erich feel better too.

Right?

He grunted as he wriggled his wrists, trying to keep the blood flowing to his hands. Maybe in the process he could loosen his wrists a little too. But Yevchenko had strapped the tape on too tightly for that. Still, he almost had to smile, imagining what Katarina would have said if she'd been here.

I read a book like this once. And she would probably tell him the story of a man who undid his wrists, pretended to be asleep, and then thunked the prison guard on the head when he came in the cell to give the man a bowl of thin soup. That's how it happened in the adventure novels.

Only not this time. Erich's hands went from tingling to pins-and-needles numb. After a few minutes he started sneezing from the moldy dust. And though he worked at it for more than a half hour, it was no good trying to chew through the layers of tape strapped across his mouth.

Captain Yevchenko paced the hallway. *How long will they keep me here?* Erich wondered. *What if DeWitt isn't around? And even if he is, will he really come to the Soviet sector, alone ... just to save me?*

He heard a faint scurrying sound, a scratching in the corner, which could mean only one thing.

In a moment he'd be nose-to-nose with a rat.

Lord, how did I get into such a mess? Erich closed his eyes and prayed, not knowing how God would answer, or whether God would think this mess he'd gotten himself into in a ruined church was a horribly sick joke. And the worst part was, it looked like it was going to get a lot worse before it got better.

If it got better. He kept his eyes squeezed shut, waiting for a nibble at his nose or the tickle of a rat whisker. Without opening his eyes he blew through his nose, over and over.

Shoo, rat! Get away!

He shivered at the thought, blew a little faster, as if burning coals had brushed his lips: *foo-foo-foo.*

Where was it? He heard the scratching sound once more and opened one eye halfway, just to check.

What? The rat had turned into a very human face belonging to the churchmouse janitor, Helmut Weiss. He peered straight at Erich through a gaping hole in the back wall and gave him a strange look. Well, anyone would have to wonder, after all that *foo*-ing. But where had the man come from?

Never mind that. Captain Yevchenko had returned to the study, washing his hands in the air once more. Weiss shook his head and melted back into the shadows.

"What are you doing in here on your face?" asked the captain, pulling Erich up by the shirt collar. "That can't be very comfortable."

He propped Erich up against the wall like a rag doll and grinned. So much for chewing through the tape on his mouth. So much for wiggling his hands free and overpowering his captor. So much for even pulling his wrists around under his feet so he'd have his hands in front of him.

So much for anything. This was obviously not one of Katarina's happy-ending adventure novels. Because in this adventure, Fred DeWitt was probably walking into a trap, Erich was the bait, and there was nothing he could do about it. Captain Yevchenko glanced at his wristwatch.

"I imagine our friend should be arriving soon."

He wasn't far off. Ten minutes later they heard footsteps coming down the hallway, crunching on broken glass. A grim-faced DeWitt—not wearing his uniform—arrived at the door just ahead of the gun barrel pointed at his back.

"You checked him for weapons, I assume?" Captain Yevchenko pointed his own pistol at DeWitt, and Pasternov, the silent bodyguard, nodded, turned on his heels, and headed back down the hallway. Yevchenko turned his attention to his new guest.

"Sergeant DeWitt!" Yevchenko greeted him like an old friend. "You're even more foolish than I dared hope. And prompt, as well."

DeWitt wasn't playing the game; he hurried over to Erich and began to pull off the tape that wound around his head. Erich didn't mind losing a little hair, not at all.

"You okay, kid?" DeWitt whispered as he removed the last of the tape and helped Erich to his feet. Erich nodded and rubbed his wrists. Yes, he was okay. But now what?

Captain Yevchenko was obviously having his fun with this.

"Imagine! Here you are in the Soviet sector without your uniform on. You'd be demoted down to corporal if your superiors found out, wouldn't you? Perhaps thrown in the brig, jailed for a few months?"

"You got that right," growled DeWitt. He wadded up a handful of electrical tape and threw it at Yevchenko's feet. "But I showed up. Now you let him go."

"Of course." Captain Yevchenko still looked amused. "I already told him I have no interest in harming anyone. He's free to leave."

Well, that was fine. But Erich decided he couldn't let Yevchenko off so easily.

"Did you hear me?" The Russian raised his voice. "Leave us!"

Still Erich didn't move, except to park himself beside DeWitt. He didn't even have to think about it. He wasn't leaving the man behind. DeWitt was beyond help over in the Soviet sector, and he'd be in deep trouble if he were found out. Erich's glance darted around the room. If he could find a piece of wood, he might have something to defend himself with.

"Listen, Yevchenko." DeWitt must have remembered the name from their last meeting. "Maybe you've got me mistaken for somebody else. I don't have anything to tell you. My enlistment's up in a couple of weeks, so I'm done with the service. I'm just a journalist, okay?"

"Just a journalist." Yevchenko spit back the words. "A journalist who happens to organize a *subversive* parachute-dropping campaign over the Soviet sector."

Subversive? As in dangerous? The way a traitor was dangerous? Erich marveled. DeWitt didn't think so, either.

"Didn't know you guys would get so bent out of shape about a little candy," he replied. "We just wanted to cheer the kids up a little."

"And you are just a journalist, you say, yet you also work as an American agent?"

"Oh, come on." DeWitt dropped his shoulders. "You guys would think my ninety-two-year-old grandmother was a spy."

"I know nothing of your grandmother. But in my country, we shoot people like you."

Erich's blood ran cold when he saw Yevchenko's finger on the trigger. And he heard in the man's voice how serious he was. Just as serious as DeWitt's low warning.

"It's time you get out of here, Erich." DeWitt didn't take his eyes off the Russian's gun. "Go home now, and don't look back. Tell your mother—"

"No." Erich wasn't sure what was going to happen. All he knew was that he could not leave now if he wanted to. Who would help them, anyway—over here? "You tell her yourself."

For once Erich didn't mean it the way it sounded. Only that he could not carry a message from a dead man. A dead man that he cared about.

"Erich!" DeWitt's voice took on a harder edge. "I didn't come over here to see you get hurt. You need to—"

"I'm sorry, DeWitt. But I'm not leaving." Erich crossed his arms and planted his feet. "Not unless it's with you."

That did it. Yevchenko glared at Erich. And Erich tried not to stare at the man silently slipping up behind Yevchenko, a broken board raised over his head like a club.

Helmut Weiss.

Yes, he'd been silent as he'd slipped up behind the captain. But the little janitor's weapon looked too big for him to hold. And as he pulled back just a little farther, ready to swing, a piece of glass snapped under his foot.

"What?" Captain Yevchenko glanced over his shoulder, probably expecting to see Wolfgang or his assistant. When he didn't, he snapped his gun hand around, too quickly for Erich to grab it. Without thinking, Erich launched himself headfirst at Captain Yevchenko, clawing and grabbing. At the same time, Helmut Weiss bellowed as he swung the club over his head.

DeWitt dived for Yevchenko's feet as the captain's gun fired wildly.

Even if he'd been shot, Erich wasn't sure he would have known right away. All he knew was a wild moment of wrestling, of grabbing the gun, another shot, yelling all around, and another dull thud as Herr Weiss connected with his target.

Then all was deathly quiet as they untangled themselves from the mess of arms and legs on the floor. Captain Yevchenko lay still on the ground, unconscious but still breathing, an angry red welt appearing on his forehead. While DeWitt got to his feet, Herr Weiss stood panting over his victim, eyes wide with horror, blood staining his shirt just above the elbow.

"Herr Weiss!" Erich blurted out. "You're shot!"

But Herr Weiss didn't move. "I've never done that kind of thing before," he gasped, ignoring the wound in his left arm. "Is he dead?"

DeWitt took charge again, and Erich felt his arm nearly pulled out of its socket as the sergeant pulled him from the floor.

"He's not dead, and neither are you," DeWitt told them. "But we all will be if we don't get out of here now!"

Still Helmut Weiss stood over the limp body of the captain.

"Listen, pal," DeWitt told him. "I don't know who you are or what you're doing here. But trust me, it's time to leave, and—"

And it seemed a very odd time to notice, but there on the floor lay the bag of coins, just out of Captain Yevchenko's reach. It must have fallen out of Erich's pocket during the fight. He reached over to pick it up. Maybe it wasn't the huge treasure he'd expected, but that didn't matter now. DeWitt watched, curious.

"God go with you, Erich," Herr Weiss said. He dropped his club then shook Erich's hand. "You know the way out."

He did. But the bodyguard must have heard shots. And what had happened to Wolfgang?

"Don't worry," Herr Weiss added as he saw Erich's expression. "Just go."

Erich nodded. And then Helmut Weiss limped into the darkness as quietly as he'd come.

Erich and DeWitt, on the other hand, weren't out of the building yet. And as footsteps thundered down the hallway toward them, closer and closer, Erich knew what to do.

"This way!" he whispered.

18

KAPITEL ACHTZEHN

CELEBRATION

THREE WEEKS LATER ...

"There, you look fine." DeWitt straightened Erich's bow tie, which in a past life had been a piece of his mother's dress. "Never seen a finer-looking best man."

Erich nearly didn't recognize himself in the mirror they'd set up in the back room of the Bergmannstrasse *missions-kirche,* the Lutheran Mission Church. Hair slicked back with a little dab of Brylcreem hair gel. Freshly pressed shirt. Long pants even, borrowed from Pastor Grunewald. Never mind that the pastor stood three inches taller and the pants had to be rolled and safety-pinned at the hem. Even his shoes looked as if they'd been given a military spit shine.

Just like DeWitt's. The American wore his brown dress uniform, creased at all the seams and fresh from the cleaners.

Same as his Air Force buddies, ten of whom had showed up early. Strange how many stood by the doors, though, their eyes on the street, arms crossed. Somehow they didn't quite look as if they were waiting for wedding guests.

Katarina, on the other hand … well, she knocked before poking her head in the door. "Are you boys ready yet?"

"Ready when you are!" answered the groom-to-be, and he gave his own tie a nervous yank. He could look as cool as a magazine ad, but Erich knew better. Under it all he could see the man's hand shaking. The jokes only helped to cover.

"You didn't invite our friends the Russkies, did you?" He winked at Erich.

"Did you want me to? Haven't seen them for the past couple of weeks."

"Just want to make sure they don't crash the party."

"Maybe they're tired of following us."

"I hope so." DeWitt checked out the window. "But hey, what kind of talk is this for a guy's wedding day?"

"The pastor's waiting," Katarina reminded them before disappearing again. At least she sounded like Katarina. The rest of the girl, Erich wasn't sure. Aunt Gerta had sewn her a yellow dress with a frilly hem and had braided her dark hair into a bun.

"I've never seen her dolled up like that," DeWitt said as he followed her out the door, then he held up a finger of warning. "You keep the guys away from her, okay?"

"Not a problem. But ... DeWitt?" He felt in his pocket for the little cup he'd been carrying around for the past few months. The only physical thing that still connected him with the memory of his father.

"Yeah?" DeWitt looked back over his shoulder.

Erich felt the knot in his stomach but held out the silver cup before he could change his mind. This would be for his mother as much as for the American, he told himself. And it was his job to take care of his mother, wasn't it? God would want him to do this ... this crazy thing. "I want you to have this."

"Are you serious?" At first DeWitt didn't seem to understand, not even as he rolled the little cup around in his hand to read the inscription:

"Presented to Rev. Ulrich Becker, Reconciliation Church, 12 June 1936." He looked up again, a question still on his face. "This belonged to your father, didn't it?"

Erich nodded.

"Why are you giving it to me?"

Erich swallowed down the lump in his throat.

"Just keeping a promise."

So DeWitt accepted the gift. The day might have been perfect, if not for the bittersweet knowledge of who was missing. Fred's Air Force friend Joe Wright stood with the groom, hardly knowing a word of German but smiling for the whole ceremony. Katarina's mother took her place next to the bride, and a handful of people from the little church joined them. But Oma was not there. That was expected, and Erich could understand why she had stayed home. Not because of her health. She'd begun to feel a little better these last few weeks. But because of who she said she would become at this ceremony.

An ex-mother-in-law, if there was such a thing.

"No, absolutely not." Mrs. Fred DeWitt put her foot down, just a few weeks after the wedding. "It's much too dangerous."

Dangerous because autumn had turned to winter and fog hung over the city nearly every morning? Or because they'd heard stories of C-54's forced off course, even fired on?

"I'm going, Mom." He looked at her and tried to sound as grown up as he could. "I have to."

"It's all right, Brigitte." DeWitt could talk her into just about anything. "I'll be with him the whole time."

She sighed and turned away, her arms crossed. Yes, she was outnumbered now, two to one, and maybe deep down she didn't mind.

"Just don't tell me anything about it afterward."

The two men grinned and headed for the door. And Erich couldn't help smiling even more as he waved at Katarina, who had come to see them off that cold Saturday afternoon, hitching a ride in Lieutenant Anderson's *Berlin Baby*. The plane looked a little grimy for all its loads of coal but still purred as loudly as ever. And this time the plane ride would be different, very different.

"Hear you're a married man now!" Jolly old Sergeant Fletcher still co-piloted the plane, even after all these months. He looked about as grimy as the rest of the C-54, but he gave them his wide smile and a slap on the back for DeWitt. "Way to go, guy."

"Pre-flight checklist!" barked the pilot. Lieutenant Anderson hadn't changed a bit, either.

"I'm on it." The sergeant pulled out his clipboard as the others settled in for a quick flight to Rhein-Main and a Frankfurt dusted with early season snow, hopeful Christmas candles in its shop windows. A few hours later Erich enjoyed the wreaths on many of the shop doors; he hadn't seen any in Berlin for years.

"So what are we going to get her?" DeWitt asked as they stepped down the newly shoveled street together. Erich stopped at a shop window to look at a box of chocolates and knew the answer.

"You doing the honors this time?" Sergeant Fletcher wanted to know, and DeWitt bowed at Erich with a flourish of his hand. The plane lurched as they approached Berlin once more.

"Wait a minute." Erich tied the corners of the next handkerchief as quickly as he could. "I still have a few more."

"Tempelhof in three minutes." Lieutenant Anderson put the plane into final approach as DeWitt opened the flare hatch. "Just make it quick, Sergeant. I don't want those things—"

"—snagging your landing gear!" Erich and DeWitt finished the pilot's warning at the same time, which made them both laugh. But the *Berlin Baby* wasn't slowing down for anybody; they'd have to work quickly. DeWitt handed the box across.

"Need some help?"

Erich shook his head no. "Not this time. But thanks."

No, not this time. He could do this. So Erich took a handful of carefully folded parachutes, ready to let loose as the wind whistled below them. He shivered as the cold December wind stiffened his fingers.

"Woo!" the sergeant chirped. "Somebody opened the barn door! A little chilly out there."

It didn't matter. This time Erich didn't think about the *other* bombers, the bombers during the war. He didn't think about anything except dropping candy to the kids on the ground. They would release right over Oma's apartment, as they'd agreed. So DeWitt glanced up through the forward windows to get their position before he started the countdown.

"*Drei, zwei, eins* ... Let it loose!"

And Erich did.

HOW IT REALLY HAPPENED

History books tell us that the Cold War began in 1948. World War 2 had ended, but the countries that had defeated Nazi Germany didn't get along. Soviet (Russian) forces took over the eastern half of Germany, while Americans, British, and French occupied the western half.

The problem was, the capital city of Berlin was stuck like an island in the middle of the Soviet territory. And about three years after the official end of fighting, the Soviets decided to seal off Allied-occupied West Berlin from the outside world. No trains or trucks would be allowed in.

What could the Allies do? Give up and go home, leaving all of Berlin to the Russians? No. Instead, the United States, Britain, and France joined to provide a massive 24/7 air supply line known as the Berlin Airlift. Between June 26, 1948, and September 30, 1949, Britain and the United States flew in 2.3 million tons of supplies to keep the western part of the city alive. Day after day they kept it up, even when no one thought it was possible.

It was a huge, and sometimes dangerous, job. And it was a hard time for the people of Berlin, who had already been through so many tough times during the war. But with the world against them, the Soviets gave up fifteen months later and once more allowed supplies in by traditional land routes.

The gum and candy drops really did happen, thanks to an American flier named Gail Halvorsen. His bravery and compassion showed the world that Americans wanted to help, any way they could.

The Reconciliation Church, the *Versöhnungskirche,* was also a real place, stuck in the no-man's-land that would grow up along the border between east and west. This border would divide a city and a people more and more over the next forty years. But the story of the people living around that remarkable church is not over—

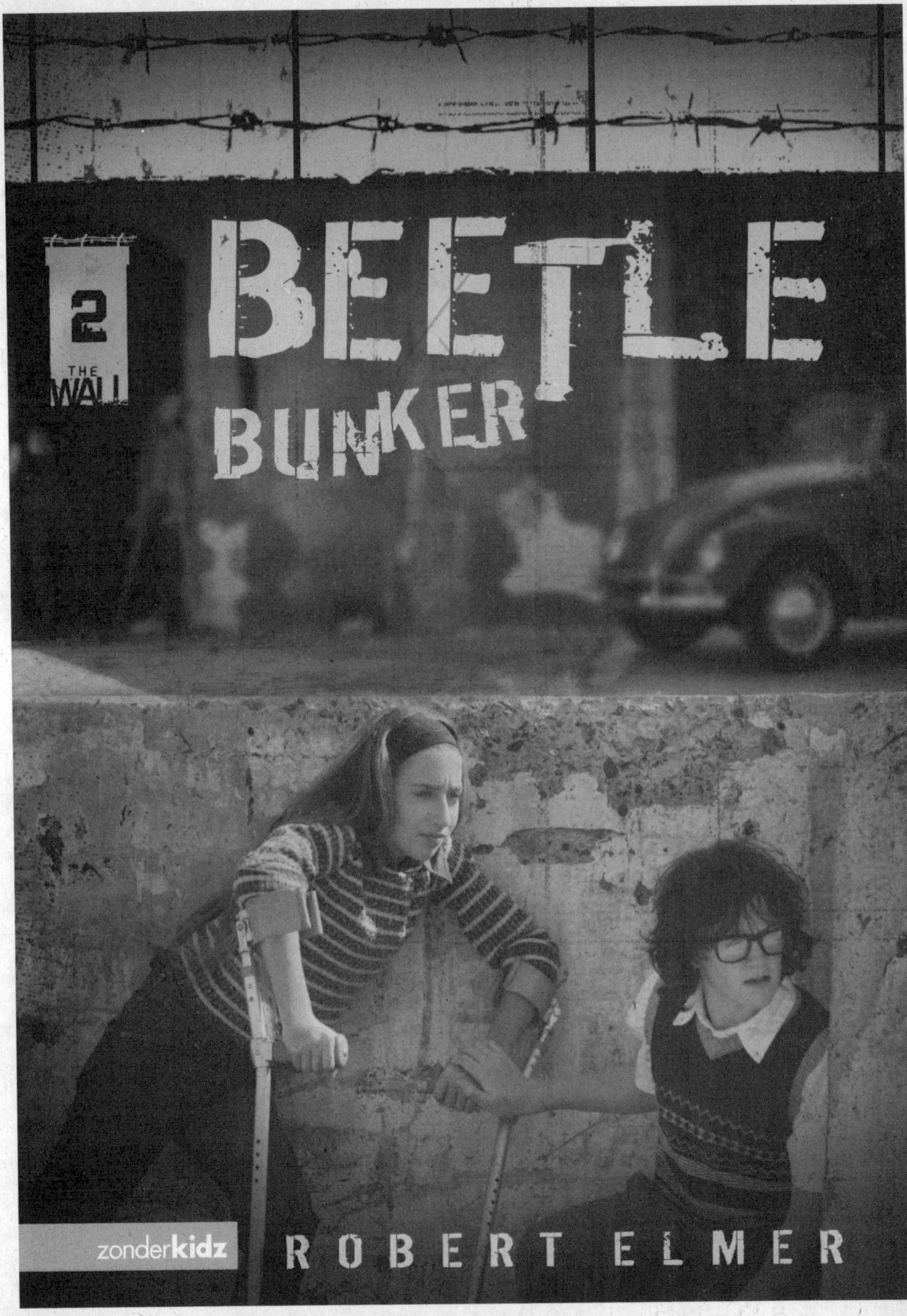

2
THE WALL
BEETLE
BUNKER
zonderkidz
ROBERT ELMER

PROLOGUE

"We will wait until you decide to stop blubbering, Sabine Becker. Until then, you can just stay in there."

Seven-year-old Sabine sat on the closet floor and shivered, holding her head in her hands.

Tomboys never cry, she told herself. But no matter what, she could not stop the sobs.

"*B-b-b-bitte*," she repeated, over and over. "P-p-p-please. I d-d-don't want to d-d-do any more today ... It hurts s-s-so much —"

But begging had never worked with Nurse Ilse. Neither had deal-making or screams or tantrums or hunger strikes. Even smiles and promises to do better later only brought a slap on the hand from the ruler Nurse Ilse carried in her apron pocket.

"We can wait as long as you like," said the nurse, "but we *will* return to your exercises." She turned the key in the lock and walked away. As her footsteps grew fainter, Sabine closed her eyes.

She didn't let herself fall asleep, though. What if Mama came while she was asleep? Nurse Ilse wouldn't wake her. She only did that in the middle of the night, when she pinched Sabine's cheek to get her attention, then forced nasty medicine down her throat. It was supposed to make her polio better.

Sabine bumped her head against the inside of the door and shivered. She prayed to her mother's Jesus and talked to her own made-up friends—like the characters from the books Mama read to her. Sometimes she wasn't sure which was which, though she would never dare admit that to Mama.

At least for a little while she was away from Nurse Ilse. Here she could escape to her pretend world, the place where she could walk and run, just like all the other kids.

Only not forever. Nurse Ilse came back a few minutes later with another threat, this one worse than locking her in a closet.

"If you continue to raise such a fuss, your mother will never be able to visit again. Never. Do you hear me?"

"I don't believe you," Sabine answered defiantly.

Maybe next time Mama will finally take me home again, Sabine thought.

Rheinsbergerstrasse. Home. To Oma's crowded apartment on Rheinsberger Street in East Berlin. Where she'd lived all her life with her mama and her ancient grandmother, Oma Poldi Becker, and her half brother, Erich. He was twenty years old and wanted to be a doctor. She tried to remember his stories about hiding on an American airplane with his cousin Katarina when he was thirteen. He even said they flew to an American air base with Sabine's father, who had been an Air Force sergeant. Sabine wasn't sure she believed it all, but of course it made her jealous of Erich. He had known her American father, while all she had were stories about his sense of humor—and about the plane crash.

If I could go home today, she decided, *I'd never complain about Onkel Heinz and Tante Gertrud again.* Her uncle and aunt had moved into Oma's apartment a couple of years ago. It made things a little crowded, but Uncle Heinz had shown her how to tell the difference between a Mercedes and a Volkswagen. She knew she wasn't supposed to care, because she was a girl, but she did anyway. He could get bossy sometimes, though, and he belched a lot. Especially when he drank beer.

Even Aunt Gertrud's ranting and smoking wouldn't seem too bad, if only—

"Out, now!" growled Nurse Ilse, startling Sabine as she unlocked the door. "You have a visitor."

Sabine blinked at the bright lights, but smiled as the nurse carried her back to bed. Wait until she could show Mama...

Her mother stood in the doorway of the hospital room only a few minutes later, her mouth and nose hidden behind a blue hospital mask but her eyes twinkling with tears. She had to wear the mask and a hospital gown just like everybody else, so she wouldn't catch Sabine's polio.

"Sabine!" Mama held out her arms as if to hug her only daughter, which of course she could not.

"I've been waiting for you all week, Mama." Sabine couldn't help grinning from ear to ear. Maybe polio could turn her legs to limp noodles, but it could not keep Mama from her weekly visit. Sabine knew that more than anything. And now it was time for the surprise she and Jesus had been working on for days, in secret, when nobody was looking.

THE WALL SERIES

In post–World War 2 Germany, tensions mount in Berlin. The former capital city is now in Soviet-controlled territory but still governed in part by the western allies, creating an isolated enclave in a hostile land. Robert Elmer's three-book series for kids unfolds against the backdrop of Cold War Berlin. Follow the teen characters in their struggle to grow up in a city brutally impacted by the Berlin Wall.

Don't miss the other exciting books in this series!

BEETLE BUNKER

In book two, it is August 1961, and without warning, a barrier erected between the east and west escalates tensions in the city. When Sabine discovers a forgotten underground bunker, it could be a way to freedom ... or to terrible danger.

Softcover 0-310-70944-X

SMUGGLER'S TREASURE

In book three of this exciting trilogy, Liesl discovers a startling secret. With the Wall continuing to separate her family, she fears she'll never know the whole story. Will her family's life be ruined by the Wall forever?

Softcover 0-310-70945-8

We want to hear from you. Please send your comments about this book to us at zreview@zondervan.com. Thank you.

ZONDERVAN.com/
AUTHORTRACKER
follow your favorite authors